Revisions of Life

CHRISTIAN CASHELLE

TO YOU

THERE COMES A TIME IN YOUR LIFE WHERE YOU
ARE GOING TO HAVE TO STOP LOOKING AT THE
NOTES OF YOUR PAST AND CREATE NEW WORDS
FOR THE CHAPTER AHEAD.

CHAPTER ONE

DONNICA

"Burning Desires by Donnica Davis is yet another letdown. The urban literature world is questioning what has happened to the author of the best-selling title *No Spaces*. Only three years since her page-turner debut, Davis' last two novels have fallen short of the hype. I wonder what the big boys at Point Set Publishing have to say about this.

"It's a disappointment really. I mean, her first novel had us thinking Davis would be around for a while. It

makes you wonder what's going on in her life to cause the quality of her writing to falter."

Donnica punched the power button on the radio before gripping the steering wheel again. She rocked back and forth in the driver's seat while trying to maintain focus on the Houston traffic ahead of her.

Her morning had started off with a phone call from her publishing company about an urgent meeting, spoiled milk in her coffee, and twenty minutes of searching for her misplaced keys. The talk radio show did not help.

"What the hell do they know?" she yelled before turning into the entrance of Point Set Publishing.

Not as tall as the other buildings around it, it still looked glorious to Donnica. Large mirror-tinted windows separated with thick strips of black went from ground to rooftop. No blades of grass were higher than the others, and no weeds disrupted the green landscaping.

She stopped at the gate next to the small wooden booth equipped with two small windows, a swinging door held open by a brick, and a small desk with two televisions sitting on it. Donnica smiled as she showed her pass and proceeded to the parking garage.

After cutting off the car's ignition, she pulled down the sun visor, flipped up the cover of the visor's mirror, and blinked her chestnut eyes to focus on her round face. As she wiggled her short, yet wide nose, the few darker freckles around her nose that she couldn't cover up with concealer came into view. Her olive complexion and the loose, dark curls of her hair reminded her of the picture on the back of her novels.

Donnica huffed, plastered on a smile, and flipped the mirror back up before sliding out of her dark green, 2009 Chevy Malibu. With the driver's door still open, she placed both hands on her belly, then inhaled through her nose and exhaled through her mouth. After collecting herself, she retrieved her things from the passenger's seat and shut the door.

Donnica's heart felt like it was throbbing in her throat as she entered the building. Amber, her publicist at Point Set, had called her in for a brief meeting. Donnica wanted to believe she didn't know what it was about, but her declining book sales gave her more than a hint.

As the double doors of the elevator opened up to the sixth floor, Donnica could remember her first ride in it just four years ago. Ten publishers had rejected her that year, and even though Amber Coley had called to set up a meeting, Donnica's confidence in *No Spaces* was dwindling.

She and Amber shared the same mind from the beginning. New in her position, Amber was ready to prove herself and help Donnica, as well. They both took a chance on each other, and they turned out to be a great team. They had even become close friends.

Mentally drained, over the last few months, Donnica felt like she couldn't even put together a sentence, let alone a novel. She didn't want to ruin Amber's career, too.

The hallway filled with a normal quiet as Donnica's heels pushed along the worn, but clean tan carpet. The open-roof ceiling cast a beam of sunlight that was famous with Houston weather. Amber's assistant looked up when Donnica rounded the corner. Her eyes bugged out as she pulled her headphones off.

"Good morning, Mrs. Davis," she said. Donnica nodded in response. "Ms. Coley said for you to go right in."

Donnica gave her a smile as a gesture of understanding and walked past her half-oval desk towards Amber's door. She knocked lightly, but didn't wait for an answer.

Amber Coley's bright green eyes were always the first things Donnica noticed. Her brown hair was pulled into a tight ponytail on the top of her head, with the exception of the bangs that lay flawlessly across her forehead.

"Morning, D," Amber greeted in a singsong tone from behind her desk as her long fingernails clicked against her laptop's keyboard.

Donnica sat down in the leather chair in front of the desk.

"A *good* morning, hopefully," Donnica responded.

Amber's thin lips turned down before she paused and closed her laptop. "The Big Boys aren't happy, D."

"The next title will be better, I promise."

"Your last two titles have failed in comparison to *No Spaces*. Point Set is not seeing a return of investment with you anymore."

Donnica's heart thumped louder as she watched Amber's

movements. Her back was straight, hands crossed, and lips tight. She figured the meeting would be centered on the topic of her failed novels, but it was beginning to sound like a termination.

"They aren't happy, and they feel like you aren't trying," Amber continued. "They've given you extensions on deadlines and advances that they can't get back. They've reached a breaking point."

"They can't break my contract can they?" Donnica asked. She sat forward in her seat, placing her right hand on the edge of Amber's desk.

Amber's chin dropped and her eyes slowly closed. "Can they?" Donnica repeated.

"I'm sorry, but Point Set has decided the fees for a breach of contract will hurt them less than taking a risk on your fifth novel."

Amber apologized with her eyes as she pushed a stack of white papers towards Donnica. Severance papers. Amber went on about a company lawyer contacting hers in the next few days to discuss the monetary issue of breaking the contract.

Donnica slid the packet into her large Coach bag, stood up, and walked out of Amber's office, almost in a robotic- like state.

Amber called after her, but Donnica kept walking.

Donnica's ears began to ring as she thought of all the late nights she spent promoting her book until they felt she deserved proper marketing. She thought of the strain her marriage sustained because she'd been writing all night to meet deadlines.

She walked past Amber's secretary, rounded the corner, and sauntered toward the elevator. As her throat constricted and her eyes began to burn, all she could think about were the countless breakfasts and lunches she had purchased at her expense to keep the staff happy and working diligently to help her during the publishing process. The halls passed by in a whirl as the heat from her emotions began behind her ears and slowly consumed her face before moving through the blood in her entire body.

Exiting the building, Donnica stepped up to the back of a black Audi A6 parked in front of a sign that read: *Reserved for Steve Point.* The sun reflected off the sign as Donnica spelled out the letters in Point Set's chief executive officer's name.

Looking down at the car with her head tilted, she could feel the heat radiating on her cheeks. There was not a flaw on the shiny black paint, and the windows were slightly tinted. It sat perfectly parked in between the two white lines.

Her nose flared before walking over to the trunk of her car and popping it. She threw her purse inside and pulled out her small Louisville Slugger. Donnica then walked briskly back to the Audi, while biting her bottom lip.

Donnica tapped the fat end of the bat along the trunk before bending her neck side to side to stretch. She exhaled before moving around to the side, swinging her arms back, and bringing the bat down on the back window. She frowned when it only cracked, a series of web-like stems branching out from the impact. Again, she swung, only harder this time, and smiled once the glass shattered.

Several different alarms went off as a delayed warning, but Donnica proceeded to smash the back windshield, back left window, and then the driver's side window. She grunted while knocking the rearview mirror off and kicking it towards the front tire. Similar to the sound of an ambulance, the alarms blared, alerting anyone around that something was happening. Her biceps began to burn from the swinging, but the adrenaline from getting even pumped through her veins.

"Ungrateful son of a bitch!" she yelled, while climbing on the hood of the car.

She could hear guards yelling as she steadied herself and raised the bat above her head. Several times she plunged the bat into the windshield. The thick glass submitted to the bat as well as her foot. Seeing the glass cave in only enraged Donnica more.

Before she could do any more damage, two guards pulled her off the Audi and slammed her against the hood. She kicked and screamed as they placed her arms behind her back. One of them even placed their knee against her shoulder to keep her in place. She groaned in pain as she felt a small piece of glass sticking her in the cheek.

Donnica cringed when she felt the cold metal of the handcuffs against her wrists. Turning her head away from the onlookers, she saw her slugger lying on the ground near the tire.

"Not a good way to end a relationship," one of the guards said as they waited for the police to detain her.

Still outraged, Donnica repeatedly threw her back into the worn cushion of the dingy backseat, while obscenities flew from her lips. The officer who was driving yelled for her to be quiet. She glared at the back of his head before shutting up.

The ride to the county jail didn't last long. With it being Donnica's first offense, she hoped she wouldn't get locked up, but once she saw her lawyer, who was also the spouse she had been separated from for the last ten months, she wished otherwise.

Jeremiah Davis walked into the building as smoothly as he

had walked into Donnica's life years ago. They had known each other since the beginning of their college years and married soon after his graduation. The time during Jeremiah's studies in law school were their best, but now they couldn't seem to find their common ground.

"Other than paying for the repairs of the car out of your severance packet, they are releasing you with community service demands," he told her. Donnica nodded as Jeremiah signed her release papers. "This is going to be all over the news. Donnica, you are way too old to be acting this reckless and childish."

"Spare me the lecture, Jeremiah. Just take me to get my car and you can get back to the office," she said, pushing past him and walking towards the double doors of the exit.

He always talked about her age as if she were some middle-aged woman trying to be younger. She wasn't even thirty yet.

She squinted under the rays of the sun while searching for Jeremiah's SUV. Once she found it, she stalked off in the direction of the vehicle and got into the passenger seat.

Jeremiah looked at his wife for a moment before starting the car. Donnica watched his side profile as he drove and instantly knew he was frustrated with her. His caramel skin had a red hue to it, and his thick eyebrows were pushed close together. His large hands gripped the steering wheel as he drove. At that moment, Donnica felt bad he had to come get her.

"Were you busy?" she asked. Her shoulders rose as she pushed her back into the comfortable leather seat.

"Nothing that can't be rescheduled."

Donnica nodded, letting silence fill the car during the rest of their ride.

Guilt resonated even more when Jeremiah drove to the car

pound and paid for Donnica's car to be released. Before handing her the keys, he checked to make sure no damage had been done to it when it was towed.

"What am I going to do about this community service?" she asked.

Jeremiah grinned before leaning against the clean, shiny white exterior of his SUV.

"I've arranged for you to teach a creative writing class at the Y," he said. Donnica's mouth dropped. "We'll go over the details next week," he told her before they went their separate ways.

We often feel the effects of failure in ripples. We are calm and content when things are working in our favor. We float through the days comfortable and satisfied with formality. When those small rings of conflict begin to stir our calm waters, we falter but don't panic. It's not until the big ones come and knock us off that we realize we've been drowning.

CHAPTER TWO

LANGSTON

"Kayla, what did I just say about calling people names?"
"Not to."
"So, stop!"
Langston Brooks glanced in his rearview mirror to see his four-year-old daughter tilt her chin down and poke her bottom lip out. She had been busy pulling on the strap of her seatbelt and telling him about her time at daycare, before he scolded her for calling little boys "ugly stink faces". Although inwardly, Langston was overjoyed she thought of boys that way.

She was as precious to him as any father would feel about his only child. She looked so much like him but held the piercing black eyes of her mother, a feature Langston still found adorable at times on Kayla's mother. Her brown curls were escaping the tamed ponytail Langston's mother had secured that morning before he took Kayla to daycare.

She had crayon marks on her white and green shirt and a ribbon missing from her left sneaker. Langston knew she'd probably taken it off herself. Kayla was his tomboy; she hated girly things, all except for Dora.

"So what should I call them?" Kayla asked. "Use their names," he replied.

"Daddy, that's not fun!" she said, throwing her small arms

up towards the roof of the car.

Langston could do nothing but laugh as he pulled up to the drive-thru of a local burger restaurant and ordered. He pushed Kayla's Dora the Explorer backpack aside and slid the bag in the passenger seat. He groaned from the looks of his car's interior. Papers were thrown all over the floor, and Kayla's toys were scattered wherever they ended up. Gym shorts, sneakers, and an extra t-shirt were also thrown across the back next to Kayla's car seat. Since he would finally have an off day tomorrow, he'd clean the car out while Kayla was at daycare.

While pulling out of the drive-thru, he glanced at his baby girl and then focused on sliding into the Houston traffic safely. He fought the urge to cuss at the thought of the conversation they were going to have. One he often dreaded, but knew was inevitable.

"Kayla, do you want to go see Mommy before we go home?" he inquired.

Kayla was quiet for a second; long enough for Langston to hear that one of his favorite R&B groups had a new song premiering on the radio.

"Do I have to?" Kayla asked.

"She might want to see you," Langston replied.

He wanted to tell her that she never had to see her mother if she didn't want. He almost doubted that his ex would even want to see her child, but he had to remind himself of the ongoing custody battle.

She mumbled that she would if he wanted her to, and Langston nodded with a small smile. He didn't want to force Kayla to see Renee, but he also didn't want Renee trying to tell her lawyer that Langston was keeping Kayla from her.

By the time Langston pulled up at Renee's apartment complex, Kayla had fallen asleep. He figured they would eat over there and then head home, but he knew once he woke Kayla up, she would be cranky and less receptive to her mother's awkwardness.

Langston threw Kayla's backpack over his shoulder before cradling her in one arm and grabbing their food in another. He walked carefully up the cracked sidewalk to the last apartment on the left and kicked at the door.

It swung open, and Renee stood there looking him up and down with narrowed eyes. Her black hair was pulled into a bun on top of her head with random strands sticking out. She had on a tight red t-shirt and a pair of black leggings.

"Are you going to let us in?" he asked. Renee rolled her eyes before stepping aside.

"You could have called first," she said, while closing and locking the door. She then spun around on her heels and looked over Langston's profile before grinning.

"I could have gone home," Langston said as he carefully laid Kayla down on Renee's faux leather couch and sat next to her.

He pulled the sandwiches out one by one before getting Kayla's food together.

"Did you bring me anything?" Renee asked. "Can you get Kay some juice before you start demanding things?" he said, pushing Kayla's cup into Renee's hands.

"I really can't stand you," she stated, stalking off towards the kitchen.

Langston sighed before turning to his daughter and slowly sitting her up. He laughed as she swung at the air and hunched her shoulders.

"You have to get up and eat, babes," he said.

Kayla's eyes rolled after she opened them. When Renee came back into the room, she sat up and moved closer to Langston.

"Hey, sleepyhead," Renee said, handing Kayla her cup.

Langston handed Renee a sandwich, and she stuck her tongue out at him.

"See, you're just childish," he commented, shaking his head.

"Dang, old man," Renee said, as she slid down in the recliner with her feet folded under her thighs. "Take a joke."

Always joking, Langston thought, but decided against saying it aloud. Instead, he ate his food and aided Kayla in eating hers.

He watched what used to be his family. Renee was twenty when she got pregnant with Kayla, and Langston was twenty-two. They were a couple then and all the way up until Kayla turned two. That's when Renee decided she hadn't been able to enjoy her first few legal years because she felt tied down.

Langston moved out of their apartment, leaving it to Renee, and found a comfortable two-bedroom dwelling a few miles away.

At first, Renee would come get Kayla every weekend and watch her while Langston was at work. Then Renee started picking her up late, or she'd come get Kayla only for Langston's mother to call him and say Renee had left her there. So, Langston put her in daycare. Soon, Renee would just visit on the weekends, and now he had to bring Kayla over to Renee's place if she was to spend any time with her mother.

He never imagined he would end up raising Kayla on his own, but once he realized Renee wasn't trying to fulfill her responsibilities as a parent anytime soon, he filed for full custody.

"Mini-Me, how was daycare?" Renee asked, after the three had been sitting in silence while eating.

Kayla looked up at her, then over at Langston and back to

Renee.

"It was okay. I painted Daddy a picture," she responded.

"What about me?" Renee asked, poking out her bottom lip just as Kayla did when she was in the car.

Langston laughed while watching Kayla act like she didn't hear what Renee said. Renee's nose flared as she tossed her burger wrapper in the empty bag.

"I got something for you," Renee said.

Her mother's announcement caused Kayla to perk up, and Renee smiled before getting up and jogging down the hall. She returned a few seconds later with a large bag. Kayla squealed when Renee reached into the bag and pulled out a brand-new Dora doll.

"I know you broke your old one the other day, so I figured we better replace it, huh?"

"Yes!" Kayla said, jumping off the couch.

She thanked Renee while hugging her. Langston just watched the show while cleaning up Kayla's mess.

Kayla went on playing with the doll, and Langston got up to throw the trash away.

"I'm the cool parent," Renee said, following Langston into the kitchen.

"Can you even call yourself that?" he asked, turning around.

He stopped when he saw how close Renee was to him. She smiled up at him before stepping even closer.

"Stop being like that with me," she said, wrapping her small arms around his waist and hugging him.

The smell of the body splash she always wore invaded his mind as he bent his head to smell it even more. It was strawberries mixed with a hint of vanilla and sugar. She bit her lip before hugging him tighter.

"Get off me, girl," he said, but made no moves to escape

her grasp.

She smiled again before standing on her toes to kiss his chin. He sighed while looking down at her.

"You don't have to be like this with me," she whispered, pushing her chest against his.

As Langston observed his ex-girlfriend, he found himself wishing she were sincere. With a Caucasian mother and black father, it was as if Renee had gotten the best of both cultures. Her smooth, light maple colored skin went perfectly with her dark almond eyes and sandy brown hair. Her round face and soft features always made Langston weak, especially her full lips, but her childish ways kept him at bay. He didn't need two daughters to raise.

Renee was always an affectionate lover. Langston never had problems being intimate with her, and that's what made it so hard to be this close to her. Renee knew if she ran her hand gently over his neck or bit his bottom lip while they kissed, she could get him to do anything she wanted. But, her neglect of their daughter had made him immune to her.

"You know how to fix it," he simply said.

Renee sighed loudly as Langston removed her arms from his waist and walked back into the living room to gather up Kayla and her things.

"Kay Kay, say bye to Mommy."

That night, after Langston got Kayla ready for bed, he sat and listened to her try to read. For her age, she knew a few words but insisted on reading the bedtime stories, which most of the time she made up from memory or from the colorful images on each page.

He thought about all the things he had to get in order to be

granted full custody of Kayla. He had a good enough
job, but he didn't want to be there forever. He wanted to
finish his degree in business, but taking care of Kayla was
already another full-time job. He always heard of fathers
running off and shying away from their responsibilities, and
he wondered what gave Renee the right to do what so many
thought he'd do.

At the age of twenty-six, he had a lot on his shoulders.

He had to make sure his record was spotless at work. He
had to make sure Kayla was smarter than any other four-
year-old at her daycare. He had to sign up for a creative
writing class at the community center in order to have
something credible on his list of accomplishments and civic
duties to present to the court.

Sometimes, he wanted to be carefree like Renee.

However, watching his daughter attempt to read until she
was sleepy but still have enough strength to wrap her tiny
arms tightly around his neck, kiss his cheek, and tell him that
he was the best was enough to make him take on any
challenge his lawyer advised him to just to keep her.

*When the world has defined what is normal, we often
question why our lives don't sync up with those around us.
We wonder why we've been picked to be different or set
aside. We try to keep up appearances, but inside, we are
desperately seeking answers. We begin to question those
around us; we choose others to blame. All the while never
realizing what's good for one man may not work for us.*

CHAPTER THREE

KARMI

And yet, I still find my way into the crevices of the next
embrace
Searching deep within myself, wanting them to pull you out
An unwelcomed emptiness that fills me, Desperately
I want you out
My nostalgic feelings of a life before your invasion are fading
I have no choice
The next one will be significantly useless, his predecessor the
same
In a past life when the innocent me was alive and well, I
would wish them all away
Through a desperate need to decipher this pain I need you
and the next one
And then the next one
The next one
But never enough

The steam in the tub rose as Karmi's copper skin tingled from the impact of the bubble bath. Her shoulders tensed as she lay back against the tub's wall and submerged her body in the water from the neck down. She exhaled and relaxed her muscles before closing her eyes. Her thick lashes tickled her skin as the mp3 player in her bedroom lulled a song through the open bathroom door. Someone had done a cover to a fallen songstress' song. Karmi usually didn't listen to rap, but the words of this song were hitting her hard.

No one wanted to be forgotten. Karmi worried about it all the time. She wondered if people she'd known in school for a few years but lost touch with thought about her.

Karmi even wondered if people she had met in stores or around town for only brief moments would remember her. Did the clerk at the grocers remember she'd paid in exact change? Did the elderly woman remember she helped her reach a can above her head in the baking aisle?

She swished around, causing small waves as she thought about her date earlier that evening. She tried to remember what it felt like in his room. She tried to remember how she navigated through it in heels after the cocktails she had.

She tried to remember his last name.

This had happened so many times that Karmi felt no shame, only resentment. She wondered if she were just as nameless to the men she had slept with as they were to her.

She dipped her slightly pointed chin into the water and inhaled the heat. The water tickled her nose and sent a small jolt of energy throughout her body. Karmi closed her eyes again and focused on the words of the rap song, which she could completely relate to. She wanted to be unforgettable.

Karmi turned to stare at as much of her reflection visible as possible from her position in the tub. Her dark emerald eyes were almost black from tiredness. Before she could examine herself further, she turned and slid all the way under the water. While looking up towards the surface of the water, her eyes began to burn as the light blurred.

She waited a few more seconds before coming up for air and finishing her bath, with her brown highlighted hair sticking to her head. Her cell phone rang before she could dry off.

After carefully sliding across the tiled floor, Karmi hopped onto the carpet of her bedroom and jogged over towards the dresser where her phone sat on the charger. She groaned upon seeing it was her mother.

"Yes, Neiva," she answered.

"No, ma'am, this is your mother, Karmiti Moore," she said.

Karmi held her laugh in. Neiva, who was half Native American and half Caucasian, hated for Karmi to call her by her first name. Occasionally, Karmi would call her that just to irritate her.

"How was Dr. Reynolds today?" "Fine."

"That's all you ever tell me," Neiva said.

"Patient/therapist confidentiality," Karmi replied, dabbing at her wet skin with a dark brown towel. It wasn't as if Karmi didn't want to tell her mother about her therapy sessions, telling her why she needed them as a different story.

"What I'll do with you, I'll never know," Neiva said.

Karmi smirked but said nothing as her mother rambled on about a dream she had about her deceased husband. Karmi always loved the stories about her dad because he was her most favorite person in the world, and he still was even ten years after his death.

"Mommy, I'm tired," Karmi said, throwing an oversized t-shirt on over her underwear.

"Still calling me *Mommy* at twenty-one."

"I'll call you tomorrow. Love you," Karmi said, ignoring her mother's coos and hanging up.

Karmi tiptoed to the hamper and threw her towel inside. She then turned off her mp3 player and muted the television before turning the light off. Just as she was about to slip in between her lavender and white sheets, her phone lit up on the nightstand.

Thinking it might be an "I love you" text from her mother, who just learned the new aged art of communication, Karmi plucked it off the table and fell back into bed. Her fingers maneuvered over the touch screen, and her smile faded as she read the text message.

It was from a guy who she had named "Hush Nightclub" after the club they'd met in. He was thinking about their night together last week and wanted to make it happen again. Karmi closed her eyes to picture his face. It flashed through a few from last week until she landed on his smooth, dark skin. She remembered the lame conversation he had, the drinks he bought her, and the trip to a motel near the club.

Her heartbeat picked up as a familiar heat ran throughout her body. She crossed her legs under the covers and wrapped one arm around her stomach. Locking her phone without replying to the message, Karmi tossed the phone to the other end of her bed before covering her eyes with her hand.

She tried to remember the words to the chant her therapist taught her to say whenever she felt the urge for sexual pleasure. It was almost like a yearning, one that Karmi usually gave in to. After a few minutes, the intensity of her want lessened and she was able to get comfortable in her bed. The light bouncing off the wall from the television lulled her to sleep.

When morning broke, Karmi erased the message from "Hush Nightclub." She made maple sugar oatmeal and scrambled eggs with cheese. While eating at her small kitchenette, Karmi looked over the summary of notes her therapist had given her the day before. It outlined the symptoms of a sexual addiction and how to identify them.

Unexplainable urges to have sexual intercourse with random men, being aroused by things average people would find ordinary—all these things hindered Karmi on a daily basis, and she had no idea how to control them.

She looked closely at the line on the paper that stated most sex addictions were triggered by a traumatic experience earlier in their lives. Incidents such as harassment, molestation, or rape seemed to be what triggered most.

Karmi quickly flipped the paper over and sighed. Her therapist suggested telling her mother, but Karmi couldn't form the words to tell Neiva. Karmi didn't even know how to sit her mother down and explain to her that the closeness of that family friend had been fabricated most of her life to protect her mother's feelings. Neiva was very sensitive about Karmi, so much so that she cried every time Karmi went to another grade in school. She almost fainted when Karmi told her that she was moving out and getting her own apartment. She had wanted to leave the state, but she knew her mother wouldn't be able to handle it, just as she wouldn't be able to handle Karmi's truth. Karmi would have to deal with this issue on her own.

She shook her head and looked toward the bottom of the notes at the recommendation for Karmi to find a hobby to consume her free time. There was a suggestion for a creative writing class at the Y. She hadn't written a poem in years. While a freshman, she had to recite a poem in

English, but her class laughed at her. She hadn't written anything since. What would she write about? Would the teacher think it was any good? She didn't think she could deal with some writer on a high horse thinking they were better than her and picking at her personal life. There was a reason why she hadn't continued her education after high school three years ago.

Karmi looked at the blinking digits on her microwave and saw she had an hour to get to work. Her mediocre job as a sales associate in a department store in the Houston Galleria was waiting on her. Two of her co-workers, whose beds she had visited, would be waiting, as well.

Karmi shook her head before pushing herself off the stool.

"Something's gotta give!" she yelled, while walking back to her room.

Before leaving for work, Karmi called the center to register for the class.

CHAPTER FOUR

DONNICA

Struggling since she dropped out of college and began to write her first novel, Donnica remembered the days when she and Jeremiah were just dating and she'd cry to him about having the words in her head but not being able to get them out. He'd encourage her and be the ear she bounced ideas off. He would even meet her at the campus library, where he'd sneak her on the computer with his school ID and password and let her type up whatever ideas she had at the time.

Donnica felt so accomplished when she finished *No Spaces*. It was about a hoarder who survived a fight with cancer and began to remove things from her life that were no longer important, including people. Donnica had become so connected with her characters that each time she received a rejection letter from a publishing company, Donnica would cry not only for her, but for her characters that may never get to live outside of her mind.

Donnica was precautious about Point Set because they were a fairly new name. Amber's infectious optimism and too many rejections gave her the push she needed to sign with them.

Her first two best sellers had not only put her on the radar in the literary world but Point Set, as well. She made Steve Point a fortune. He owed her more than a severance package for cutting her contract. She couldn't understand why she had done what she did to his car. Donnica just didn't know what to do with her anger.

As a result, they took almost half of her severance package, and Donnica had to teach the creative writing class for a little over three months. It was one night a week for two hours. Jeremiah said it was very generous of the judge.

Donnica had a meeting with the manager of the YWCA. She parked her Malibu in the parking lot across the street and looked up at the building. It couldn't have been more than three stories. The lower tan bricks were covered with dark patches of mud, stale gum, and weathered by rain. Most of the windows on the second

floor had small paintings and drawings on various colors of construction paper taped across them. The tinted glass doors swung back and forth as people passed through them.

Donnica listened to a few songs on the radio before shutting the engine off and getting out. The hot Houston air met her face in a rush as she looked both ways and jogged across the street. Since she had on a pair of red, gray, and white sneakers, light denim Capri pants, and a red short-sleeve polo, it was easy for her to jog up the cracked stairs, avoiding any small pits that would hinder her stride.

Donnica's body welcomed the cool air as she passed through the same doors she had been watching.

There was a long, rounded desk with a few people's heads peeking above it. There were stacks of papers spread across it with schedules for workout classes and other workshops. Donnica even noticed a brochure for an upcoming writing workshop.

"Can I help you?" a man asked, smiling.

Donnica smiled back at the older man and stepped closer to his spot at the desk.

"Hi, I'm Donnica Davis. I have a meeting with Mr. James," she said.

He nodded before looking down at a piece of paper and then back up at Donnica.

"Yes, yes. If you go right up those stairs to the third floor and take a right, Mr. James is in the gym. He's waiting for you."

Donnica nodded before turning towards the stairs.

She rolled her eyes upon realizing she couldn't jog up these steps like she had done the ones outside. When she got to the gym, she slowly pushed the door open to make as little noise as possible and looked inside. There were only a few girls and boys playing basketball on the far end. Donnica stepped inside and pressed her butt to the door, slowly stepping forward to close it silently. Her footing slipped a little, she stumbled forward, and the heavy door closed with a thud.

Although the children didn't seem to be bothered, Donnica looked up to see a man and woman in a corner watching her. The man smiled, then turned to say something to the woman before standing up and walking towards her.

"Mrs. Davis?" he asked.

Donnica nodded and he extended his right hand. "Nice to meet you. I'm Ron James."

"Nice to meet you, too," Donnica said, shaking his hand.

"I was just speaking with one of our counselors, but we can head to my office, if that's okay with you?" he asked.

Donnica gave him a tight-lipped smile and held her hands out with her palms facing up. "Lead the way."

Donnica followed Ron until they reached a small office around the corner from the gym. It was very cluttered. Donnica almost snickered, feeling as if she had seen this on an episode of *Hoarders* when she was researching her first novel. Ron had papers scattered all over his desk and open boxes of files stacked around his desk. He removed a stack of papers from the chair in front of his desk, allowing Donnica to sit.

"I'm going to be honest, Mrs. Davis. I haven't read any of your novels," Ron said with his chin tilted and his lips tucked in.

Donnica smiled. "It's okay."

"But," he continued, "your lawyer spoke highly of your work to our workshop coordinator, and I take it that she was already a fan."

"Great."

"However, I also know this was mandated by a judge, which means you are not here on your own accord."

"Let me explain," Donnica started, but Ron held his hand up and smiled.

"No need. We get a lot of volunteers that way. I just want to set the ground rule that not giving this your all will not only hurt those who have signed up for this workshop, but also my evaluation of you that the courts have mandated I do at the end of your hours."

Donnica squinted before nodding slowly, understanding that Ron didn't want her to treat this class as something that wasn't important, even if it wasn't to her.

"Will I be monitored?" she asked, sitting up and crossing her legs.

"Not every week, no," he said.

So how will you know what I do? Donnica thought, nodding as Ron continued.

"So far we have six people registered. We have a tentative date of September 12th to start, so that gives you a few weeks to prepare," Ron said, handing a stack of stapled papers to Donnica, who cringed at the memory of her last day at Point Set. "You haven't finished school, is that correct?"

"No, but I'm well aware of how creative writing classes go," she told him.

"Well, try to refrain from letting the students know that. Just give them the accolades of your career."

"Will do," Donnica replied.

She sighed as Ron continued going over the guidelines of the center and what Donnica would be expected to do. She couldn't get out of there quick enough.

On her way home, Donnica decided to stop by Jeremiah's new apartment to tell him how it went. She still couldn't get used to the idea that they were living separate lives, but she wouldn't bring herself to file for a divorce either.

She hated when he was right. Ever since last week, she had been the topic on all the Houston radio talk shows. There was even a story on the news channel. She had been getting emails from colleagues asking if she was okay, and some were even bold enough to critique her last novel and tell her where she went wrong.

Yet, she still didn't know.

Someone's car was parked in the usual spot she occupied when visiting Jeremiah. Every now and then she would come and cook for him, and they would have a civil dinner together that didn't involve formalities or proper etiquette for separated spouses.

Donnica slid her car into a nearby parking spot and jogged over to Jeremiah's door. It took him a few minutes to answer the bell.

"Donnica, I was just about to head out," he said, holding the door open.

Ignoring him, Donnica pushed past him and into his living room.

"You will not believe those people at the Y, Jay," Donnica said, flopping down on his leather couch. The whoosh sound it made filled the room before silence. "Where are you going?" she finally asked.

"Out," he said, closing the front door but not moving from his spot.

Donnica watched him through her black eyes as he moved around rearranging things.

"Out where?" she inquired, noticing his attire.

He was dressed a lot more casual than his usual suit. "Do you have on sneakers?" Donnica asked, sitting up from the couch.

"I have a lunch date…meeting," Jeremiah said.

Donnica bit her lip as her light skin turned hot and her neck tensed.

"The hell? A date?" she asked.

Donnica slid back on the couch, probably interrupting his plans but not caring at the moment. She needed him. He did not move to sit down. Instead, he kept pacing near the door.

"It's nothing serious. I'm just catching up with an old friend who may need some legal advice. I meant to say meeting."

"No, you meant what you said. When did we discuss us dating?" Donnica said.

Jeremiah glanced at her and laughed.

"We didn't discuss you throwing me out because you felt I wasn't there for you ten months ago, so what do we have to discuss now?"

Donnica noticed Jeremiah's straight posture, his shoulders back and his feet planted firmly. The evidence of a losing battle showed itself, and Donnica despised it.

"Can we talk?" she asked, pushing her sneakers into his carpeted floor and lifting off the couch with her palms. She walked towards Jeremiah, but he crossed his arms and shook his head.

"Go home, Donnica."

Donnica slumped over the island counter in her dark kitchen. Without turning the light on, she followed the evening's glow from the bay window to the freezer where a half empty bottle of vodka chilled.

She grabbed a bottle of cranberry juice along with a glass and headed out of the kitchen. An open door behind the staircase led to Donnica's haven—her office.

A bookshelf wrapped around all but one of the walls with various authors all grouped by genre. The ones she liked to reread were in the front. Her desk sat in front of the only wall to hold a window with maroon drapes.

Besides a file cabinet that was pushed against the side of the desk, there was a lamp and a chair. The only other thing in her office was a small loveseat that matched the couch in her living room.

Donnica hunched over on the floor and sat in front of her desk, pressing her back against the wood. She mixed the two drinks before downing the first glass and pouring another. Her latest novel wasn't selling, and she had almost gone through her advance for it. On top of that, her publicist had been calling her to do damage control, she had to create a plan for the creative writing class, and now she had to worry about Jeremiah finding someone else.

After finishing off the bottle, Donnica's eyes couldn't focus on the painting next to her office door. She squinted but laughed when the familiar pound of a headache surfaced.

"That'll do it," she said, slinging the bottle across the floor.

Pulling her cell phone from her pocket, she tried to call Jeremiah to no avail. Donnica groaned before resting her head on the carpet and closing her eyes.

Then came her time to teach.

Donnica tried to keep herself in the task at hand, but she hadn't talked to Jeremiah in weeks, not since the day she showed up at his place. She hadn't called him either, but she wanted him to reach out to her to see if he even cared.

Now she was sitting in the designated room of the community center waiting on her class to start. Donnica sat back in the wooden chair and smoothed out her blouse. She had come in early to prepare, writing her name on the chalkboard and the question *"What is creative writing?"* underneath it.

Donnica felt like an elementary school teacher. Although given a list of the registered participants, she couldn't tell the ages of the students by their names. Seeing as the class started at five o'clock on Wednesday nights, Donnica realized she wasn't sure if they were school age or adults. She sighed before shifting through the copies she just made in the office.

Around a quarter until five, someone came through the door and asked if they were in the right place.

"Seems like it," Donnica said, standing up to walk around the desk and sit on the end of it as a few more people filed in.

At the correct time, seven people were there, but there were nine names on her list. Most of them seemed to be adults. A few looked very young, but their attire may have indicated they were older than their physical appearance. Donnica glanced at each one, wondering in her head if she could place each name with a face without asking until she noticed they were all staring back at her.

"Hi. Welcome to your creative writing workshop.

Let me start off by introducing myself. I'm…"

"Donnica Davis," one of the young faced girls spoke up with a smile.

Donnica turned towards her and nodded. "I love your books."

Donnica tried not to smile while thanking her. She wondered which books she was referring to but decided not to venture into her own pleasures at the moment. Before she could respond, the door creaked open and a tall, black man entered. His shoulders slumped over once he realized all eyes were on him.

"Sorry I'm late. I was dropping…"

He started to explain, but Donnica cut him off by walking back around her desk.

"Please don't make it a habit. Have a seat."

A desk shifted under his weight as Donnica picked up the stack of papers and proceeded to pass them out.

"Have any of you taken previous writing classes?" Donnica asked.

Only two people raised their hands.

"*Great*," she thought. "*Back to basics.*"

"What I just passed out was a tentative schedule for the first month and a half, during which I will decide how to proceed with the last half based on your abilities. Before we get into anything heavy, why don't we get introductions out the way?"

One by one, they gave their name and a short explanation of why they had taken the class. Most of them said it was out of interest. The two that sparked her interest were the one who expressed liking her books, Karmi, who said it was recommendation, and the late man, Langston, who said the same thing.

Donnica knew it was more to each of their stories and wondered how she could find out more. It could lead to a more eventful three months was how she saw it.

Karmi Moore stumbled over her words, but she sat with her back high and her wild curls covering her face. She kept a pair of dark glasses on most of the time, but when she addressed the class, she slid them above her forehead, using them to pull back her tresses. She announced her attendance was a recommendation from her doctor.

Donnica only knew of one type of doctor that would recommend a creative writing course as a form of medication.

Langston Brooks was lost. Donnica noticed that every time she used a technical writing term, his eyebrows would lower in confusion. He spoke low with disinterest until he mentioned his daughter. His eyes sparked as he gave a few details of his most prized possession. Donnica couldn't understand why someone would recommend him to come to the class, but she didn't mind.

They got into talking about their favorite authors. There was a mix from Eric Jerome Dickey, Mary Higgins Clark, and even older authors such as Sylvia Path. Donnica was impressed. She was well read. She loved to read any book she could get her hands on, so she was glad she'd be able to converse with them about that and even get some suggestions on new titles to pick up. Before she knew it, the first two-hour class was over.

Donnica sighed as she moved across the empty classroom, making sure it was the way she had found it. She straightened the desks and made sure each chair was pushed in under it. Donnica then erased her name from the chalkboard.

She pulled her class log out of her bag and made the journey up to Ron's office. He was headed out for the evening himself.

"Oh, Mrs. Davis, how did the first night go?" "Good

actually," she said. "Was wondering if you could sign this for me?" Donnica asked, holding the paper up.

"I see," he said, sliding his hand behind it for support. He pulled the pen from his shirt pocket and signed it quickly. "How about we sign monthly so we won't have to take up too much time each week?" he suggested.

"That's fine," Donnica replied.

Ron nodded and slid past her down the hallway.

Donnica wondered why he seemed not to want to be around her much. He was very short with her. Donnica wasn't used to being an outcast. Ever since she began putting her picture on the back of her novels, she would get random people stopping her to ask if she were Donnica Davis. It wasn't much attention, but she liked it.

Are people really that disturbed by what I've done? she wondered.

Donnica's usual forty-five-minute ride home was completed in thirty. She dropped her things at the door and jogged to her laptop that sat idly open on her dining room table in the midst of bills, junk mail, and local advertisements. After logging on, Donnica went to Google and typed in her name.

There were a few news stories about her rage at Point Set Publishing. Some even had pictures of Steve's car post Donnica's slugger. Blogs were asking people what they thought. Donnica's heart thumped as she read the strangers' opinions of her.

One anonymous user said she was a sad case for a has-been. One went as far as to say none of her novels were worth reading, not even her two best sellers. Donnica couldn't help but laugh when a racist comment came up.

She slammed her laptop shut, pushed herself away from the table, but didn't get up from the chair. After a few moments, Donnica went upstairs to bed.

The next day, Donnica pulled into the parking space next to Jeremiah's empty one and sighed. She tapped her fingers against the steering wheel before looking up at the roof of her car. She had been sitting at home writing all day but couldn't fill one page with anything good. She needed to talk to him, and she knew he would be home soon.

With gas prices so high, Donnica turned the ignition off, got out, and sat on the trunk. The Houston heat puffed against her face. Small drops of sweat beaded up on her forehead. She looked around the small grassy field and saw some of Jeremiah's neighbors' kids running through a few sprinklers.

Her heart thumped as Jeremiah's car turned into the lot. She watched his tires slow as he passed her and into his space.

Donnica hopped off the trunk as Jeremiah got out of his car. He sighed before shaking his head, but Donnica threw her hands up in surrender.

"I just want to talk, Jeremiah, please."

"I don't have time to talk to you, D. I'm in between meetings."

"Well, when are we going to talk then? We can't keep ignoring the issues we have."

"That's what you wanted, right?"

Donnica stopped in front of him and dropped her arms to her side. She recognized the change in his demeanor and wondered what she had done to cause it. A few weeks ago they were fine, all things considered. She swallowed and tried not to cry in front of him. She needed comfort, and his was all she would accept.

Her family was from Missouri and decided to stay there when Donnica bought her one-way flight ticket to Texas. The lit scene in the Midwest had leveled out with historical nonfiction and didn't leave much room for Donnica's style of writing. She sold them with the idea of college to pay for the ticket. She did enroll, but at the time, she had no intentions of finishing. She met Jeremiah and he believed in her dream.

"When can we talk?"

"When I'm not busy I'll come and talk to you."

Feelings of defeat washed over Donnica's sullen face as she nodded and headed back to her car.

People often say when it rains, it pours. Others say if it's not one thing it's another. Some may even feel like everything goes from bad to worse right before your eyes. When the cause of turmoil shows the effects of a downpour, it doesn't bring along new problems. It just reveals those that were already there.

CHAPTER FIVE

LANGSTON

Steel Supply wasn't a gruesome place where one would slave over hot metals in dangerous conditions all day. It was actually just a large warehouse presented as a storefront where residential and commercial needs could be met. A large gray structure, it had ceiling-to-floor windows a few feet around the double doors and large four panel windows around the building. When the lights were on, you could almost see everything in the store when you walked up to the front door.

Customer service wasn't the best, but the employees were knowledgeable about all types of projects to aid the clientele.

Most days, Langston worked in the back actually cutting and packaging the steel that was presented on the sales floor. If he was lucky enough and someone called in sick, his boss would allow him to work the floor, but it wasn't often.

Today he was in his usual workspace, binding up small, steel pipes to get them ready for sale. He had been on the early shift ever since Kayla started daycare, but it still was not easy for him to wake up so early to be at work by seven. The only good thing about that was he got off in time to pick Kayla up from daycare and spend the rest of the day with her, no matter how tired he was.

Langston tried to focus on keeping the binding straight, but his mind kept wandering to the short story he was attempting to write for Donnica's class. He had to admit he found writing a little more interesting than he thought he would. He hadn't read many books lately, but after the first class, he made a trip to the bookstore and picked up a few while getting some children's books for Kayla.

He picked up one by Omar Tyree and another by Eric Jerome Dickey but couldn't decide on which to read first. His short story was about a trip he had taken with his dad as a young boy and how he wanted to be able to do a lot of those things with Kayla. He wasn't sure how to finish it, so he planned on reading a little more of someone else's work to get some ideas.

He thought about the class and some of the people in it, how they were all so different from each other.

Langston thought he'd be the only male, but there were three others—one also black—and that made him feel a little more at ease about following his lawyer's suggestion to join it.

Just after he finished a full pallet to be moved to the sales floor, Langston's shift came to an end. He rushed to the back room to clock out so he would be on time to pick Kayla up. Every ten minutes he was late would cost him at the end of the week.

He was glad Kayla had been worn out at daycare. It didn't take much for her to go down for a nap, which gave him more time to himself.

Langston fell into a comfortable position on the couch and turned to the first page of Omar Tyree's book. He had gotten through the first chapter, when his phone rang. He shook his head when his phone called out his brother's name, knowing that the next few minutes or so would be nothing short of ridiculous.

"Bro!"

"What's up, Jus?" Langston asked.

"Wondering what my bum brother is up to?" Claude joked. Langston laughed.

Claude Justin had always been the reckless, youngest Brooks. Their sister, Jessie, was the middle child. While in college, their mother was in love with anything from the Harlem Renaissance. Claude didn't like his name, so a lot of people called him Justin. Langston shortened that to Jus.

"Kayla's sleep, so I'm chilling," Langston told him. "Bro, you need to move around with me tonight," Jus said, as if he hadn't heard Langston's answer. "I'm promoting at a few clubs tonight, and I know you need a drink."

"Didn't you hear me say I got Kay?"

"Call that midget to come get her seed, dude!"

"I could care less what you call Renee right now, but that seed is your niece," Langston said, closing the book after securing his page with an opened bill and putting the book down on his coffee table.

"And I love her like my own," Jus said. "Just call her! Kay's hers, too."

Langston had heard this speech from everyone on more occasions than he'd love to admit. It was almost as if he was encouraged to run around and club hop with his younger brother than do what he was doing, which was taking care of his responsibility.

Jus was twenty-two and still in college for communications. In the meantime, he had been using his popularity to make money promoting the nightlife of Houston. Most of the time it was college parties, but every now and then he would get a bigger club to hire him.

Langston was actually proud that he had made a positive thing out of clubbing. Why shouldn't he? He was young with no girlfriend and no kids. He didn't need his brother to be burdened with the real world just yet.

"Or call Ma. She's at home. I just talked to her," Jus went on, trying to give Langston as many options for the night as he could.

"And I have to work tomorrow," Langston said, looking around the room into the quiet, wondering when was the last time he'd went out.

"Man, just shut up and call somebody. I'm picking you up at nine."

Before Langston could come up with another excuse, Jus ended the call.

Langston sighed before leaning back on the sofa. He could almost feel the burning liquid of a drink sliding down his throat. He rubbed his neck a little before grabbing his phone. He stopped at "Mom" but decided to keep going until he got to Jessie's number.

"Hey, honey," Jessie answered. "What's up?" "Jess, you busy tonight?" Langston asked.

"Other than washing your nephew's hair, no, sir. What's up?"

"Jus is bugging me to go to some clubs with him. I was wondering if you were up for Kay tonight?" he said, sighing. "I could really use a break."

When Jessie laughed, Langston asked her, "What's funny?"

"Justin called me before he called you, and I swore to him that you would say no. Guess I lost ten bucks," she said, still laughing. Langston rolled his eyes, not amused with his younger siblings at the moment.

"So is that a yes?"

"I surely do miss my niece," Jessie said and Langston smiled. "You're bringing her over?"

"Yeah. I won't make you pack up Ashton like that." "I

would have made Ryan do it," Jessie said.

Langston knew she was telling the truth because Jessie's husband did everything for her. They had been married for five years, and Langston's nephew, Ashton, was the same age as Kayla.

"No. I'll drop her off after I get her together," Langston said, springing up to his feet. The anticipation of not having any responsibilities for the night was building.

"Well, don't feed her. I'm cooking. Bye!"

Langston ended his call with his sister and headed to pack Kayla's backpack with what she would need. When he went into her room, she was sprawled across her bed with her legs crossed, one arm over her belly and the other twisting her ear. Her eyes were glued to her television where Dora was playing. It was a DVD that Langston kept in the player so she could just hit *Play* when she wanted to watch it.

She turned and smiled at him before patting the little empty space on her bed. Langston shook his head and smiled before sitting next to her.

"Rojo is red right?" she asked.

Langston nodded and gave her a high-five.

"Guess who you get to have a sleepover with tonight?" he asked.

Kayla's eyebrows came closer, but she didn't say anything.

"Ashton."

Kayla playfully rolled her eyes and said, "He ate my ice cream last time he was over here."

Langston laughed. "Well, Ti-Ti Jessie misses you.

So, she's going to keep you tonight while I hang with Uncle Jus," he said, then held his breath waiting for her reaction. Kayla wrinkled her nose before turning back to her show.

"That's cool," she responded. "Ti-Ti does my hair better than you anyway."

Langston looked at her for a second before laughing and gently tapping her head. She giggled as he got up to pack her bag.

After Langston dropped Kayla off, he returned home to change. He opted for a black and blue striped, short-sleeve, button-down shirt with dark denim jeans and sneakers that matched his shirt. He brushed over his hair, glad he had gotten a haircut a few days before, and debated on whether or not to wear his favorite watch. He didn't want to lose something so expensive in a club, so he decided against it.

True to his word, Jus came and picked Langston up at nine. His truck was packed with guys, but he had left the passenger seat vacant for Langston. The loud music thumped against Langston's chest as he got in and shut the door.

"Somebody take a picture of this!" Jus said, patting Langston on his shoulder.

A few guys laughed as Langston threw Jus's hand off of his shoulder and shook his head.

"Cut it out, Jus," Langston said.

His little brother smiled before handing him a small, tinted bottle. "Last one in the car takes the first shot."

Langston took the bottle, unscrewed the cap, and took the equivalent of a double shot. Jus stared him down, and Langston looked back at him with a straight face. The guys in the car hooted as Jus nodded his approval. Langston handed him the bottle back as he drove off.

"That's what I'm talking about!" Jus shouted.

Langston let the slow burn in his throat excite him for upcoming events of the night. Smiling, he bobbed his head to whatever song played.

He needed a night off.

The first two clubs weren't what Langston expected. They were ushered into the exclusive spots so Jus could announce his presence and hype up the crowd. Everyone with them was given free drinks and crowded around, but the third club was different.

He wasn't sure if it was the atmosphere or the previous drinks that had been working in his blood, but he was feeling everything about that club.

The main light was low, but there were red, yellow, and blue lights moving viciously over the dance floor. The walkway curved around the entrance to the first bar across from a long ottoman that separated a few round tables from the bar. Past that, the dance floor fell down into a circle; above were a few steps with rails all around it and the same rounded tables overlooking the dance floor. There was a large stage against the wall where several men were sprinkling water from open water bottles on to the people closest to the stage.

Jus pulled Langston near the stage. He would have gone up with Jus, but a short Latina with thick hips pushed close against his chest with a smile.

A silent agreement between them, Langston wrapped his arms loosely around her waist as she twisted and turned her back to him. She dipped her hips against his leg, and he dipped to meet her rhythm. She turned her head to look at him and smiled. He glanced at Jus who had just been announced. He winked at Langston before giving his attention and energy to the crowd.

After two songs, the small woman turned back around.

Her big, pretty eyes disappeared as she batted her lashes and gripped his shirt to bring him to her level.

"Thanks for the dance, papi," she yelled into his ear, her cheek pressed against his.

He squeezed her sides a little before letting her go. She smiled and walked away. Woman after woman approached him for a dance. A few gave him their numbers, while one with sparkling eyes convinced him to sit at the bar so she could buy him a drink.

"I didn't think women these days bought drinks for guys," he said.

"I don't buy drinks for guys. I bought *you* one," she said. "Alisha."

"Langston."

"As in Hughes?"

"Mom thing."

Alisha laughed, and Langston thought he saw Renee's smile. He took a swig of his drink after clearing his throat.

"Justin's your brother?" she asked. He nodded yet frowned. "You guys look alike."

"You know him?"

"I work here," Alisha said. Langston nodded and relaxed. "I know this is your first time here. I didn't want to miss you."

"You're pretty bold," Langston replied.

"I'm a big girl."

Langston couldn't help but look over Alisha. She was almost his height with the heels she wore. She wore flower-designed black tights that disappeared under the dark red dress that crossed on her upper back and faded into black on the short sleeves. Her brown hair had small streaks of blonde and pulled tightly into a bun on the top of her head. The hairstyle seemed to be a trend now.

"See something nice?" she asked, leaning over to catch his eyes with hers.

Langston just smiled and finished his drink.

They danced to a few songs before Jus came to find him to leave. Langston turned to Alisha and demanded her number. She smiled and complied.

"Now tell your little brother he's the best and the sole cause of the best night you've had in months," Jus said, as he pulled up in front of Langston's house at almost four o'clock that morning.

"I won't say all that," Langston said, "but I did have fun."

Never underestimate the power your words have on others. You may be discouraged, depressed, or feeling unmotivated, but braving through those hard times is showing someone around you that it's okay to be the way they are. You may have something that doesn't make sense to you, and you may want to crumble it up and throw it away in shame. There's someone who can straighten out that paper and breathe life into those same words you trashed.

CHAPTER SIX

KARMI

*In its worn fabric, my heart is calm I cannot feel the cold
around me
Every wrinkle satisfies a soothing memory Every tear is
a triumph of my own
Its purple stitching speaks life into my breathless being
Revealing the assuring power of its comfort My father's
spirit is wrapped up in that blanket My innocence is
wrapped up in that blanket
I am at peace, wrapped up in that blanket I know in
here, his hands cannot touch me*

Karmi looked up at the tiles on the ceiling of her therapist's office. She twisted her thighs against the cool leather and counted each tile separately in her head while Dr. Reynolds read from her recently published book. It was a passage about releasing the cause of an addiction to actually be freed from the addiction itself.

"I have gotten over it," Karmi spoke, cutting Dr. Reynolds off. "I've forgiven him."

"Do you really believe that?" Dr. Reynolds asked.

Karmi violently nodded her head. "Karmiti, be serious right

now."

Karmi grimaced at her full name. She had repeatedly asked Dr. Reynolds to call her Karmi, but Dr. Reynolds always made it a point to say each syllable in her name.

"I…I prayed about it."

"Have you seen him since you prayed about it?" Dr. Reynolds asked. Karmi shook her head. "How do you think you'd react to him today? If you saw him walking past this office as you leave, how would you react?"

Karmi opened her mouth to say she wouldn't feel anything and would probably walk right past him.

Although the words floated around in her mind, they never made it to the surface, and Karmi knew it was because it was a lie. She had always imagined what she'd say to him, how he'd look, if she'd even acknowledge him at all, and she had always come to one conclusion.

"I honestly don't know," she said, her voice cracking. She rolled her eyes in self-annoyance. She hated crying in Dr. Reynolds' office.

"You ready to tell me who he is?"

Silence filled the room as Karmi began to count the tiles again. She counted to fifteen and stopped. That was how old she was when she finally realized what was happening to her was wrong, very wrong.

He was always around. He was always doing favors for her mom and dad, picking her up from school when they were busy. His car always smelled of his cologne with a cinnamon twist from the mints stuffed in the ashtray. He listened to jazz music on a regular. Karmi always heard it in her head after he'd let her out in front of her home, after he'd stopped near the park, slid down into his seat, and reached for her hands to touch him.

"He started when I was twelve." "Who started when you were twelve?" "Hassun, my dad's college buddy."

"What did Hassun start when you were twelve?"

Karmi's throat burned as she tried to keep her focus on the ceiling tiles, but they began to blur together. His deep, scratchy voice fell in her ears so heavy that she jerked her head to the left, only seeing a bookcase there. She shut her eyes tight, inhaled, and held it.

"Exhale, Karmi."

She pushed the air through her mouth and pushed her heels into the cushion of the chaise. She had taken her shoes off to get comfortable earlier.

"He started touching me. At first, it was just my hair and my face, but then he moved on to other things, things I wasn't familiar with at that age," Karmi said as her skin burned.

She wanted to crawl into her tub and stay there for hours like she used to do whenever Hassun turned her loose.

"He told me that he was teaching me things my dad never would, and he was the only one who could because he was the same as us."

"You mean Native American?" Dr. Reynolds asked.

Karmi nodded. Her body heat had not returned to normal. Instead, she had started to sweat. Her ears deafened as the tension in her shoulders caused her to roll her neck. Karmi felt uncomfortable, dirty.

"I don't want to talk about him anymore," Karmi blurted out.

"It's okay. We don't have to. You did really good."

"*But what did I do?*" Karmi thought. "*I let it happen for three years without realizing I was being molested.*"

"It's not an easy thing to relive a horrible memory," Dr. Reynolds stated.

"So why are you making me?" Karmi asked through tight lips. She glared at her therapist who sat in a low, leather chair on the right of her.

"Have you had any setbacks this week?" Dr. Reynolds called Karmi's sexual exploits "setbacks." Karmi twisted her fingers in the air before lying to Dr. Reynolds, saying she had not.

"How is the writing class going?"

"We've only had one, but I recognized the teacher from her work. So, it doesn't seem to be all bad," Karmi said, remembering how in awe she was to meet someone she had seen on the back of books in her own home.

"Have you written anything yet?" "I wrote a poem."

"About?"

"Sex."

The short groan that came from Dr. Reynolds caused Karmi to sit up and frown.

"What? It's just a poem!"

"That's not the point. I recommended the class to get your mind off of sexual experiences. Writing about it is not going to help you."

"Well what am I supposed to write about?" Karmi asked.

"Do you remember telling me that sex only pacifies you? That you enjoy it but feel empty afterwards?" she asked, not waiting for a reply. "Write about what makes you happy even after it's done."

Karmi ran through her brain to find something Dr. Reynolds would approve of. She couldn't think of any places or people, but one inanimate object came to mind.

"There's a blanket," Karmi said.

Dr. Reynolds smiled.

"It's not like a child's blanket or anything, but my Nana made it."

"Go on."

"My mom used to use it as decoration on the couch, but I would always take it off, go into the corner of my bedroom, and wrap myself in it."

"What about after your times with Hassun?" "Definitely after those times. I'd fall asleep in that corner with that blanket," Karmi said. "It had a lot of vibrant oranges, but it had a weird purple stitching all around it. It's very warm."

"Do you still have the blanket?" Dr. Reynolds asked. "No, my mom does," Karmi replied.

Dr. Reynolds nodded and scribbled away in her notebook.

"That made me happy."

"Well, write about that then," Dr. Reynolds said. "Start there."

"Neiva, you home?" Karmi asked, walking through the threshold of her mother's home.

She thanked God every time she came there that it wasn't her childhood home. Neiva moved out of it after Karmi's dad died.

"Stop calling me that!" Karmi heard from the back.

She jogged through the house, turned into her mother's bedroom, and dove on the bed. Neiva barked something in her native language as Karmi snuggled into her pillow.

"How was work?"

"Damaging," Karmi responded.

"Stop being so emotional," Neiva said, walking into her room from the adjoining bathroom.

Karmi smiled at her mother. She had been losing weight, but her full figure fit her round face.

Neiva swatted at Karmi's leg. "Get up, child," she commanded, regaining her position on the bed.

Karmi waited until Neiva was comfortable before laying her head in Neiva's lap, facing her feet. Neiva instinctively began to part Karmi's hair and massage her scalp. Karmi relaxed as her mother hummed.

"Do you still have Nana's blanket?" Karmi asked. "The one with the purple stitch?"

"Um hum, it's in the guest room." "Can I have it?"

"You want it?"

"Yes, ma'am."

"Get it before you leave."

Karmi nodded before the conversation continued.

CHAPTER SEVEN

DONNICA

The third week of her class and Donnica had a routine. She had been searching through the textbooks she'd kept while in school for writing exercises or good essays to share.

The few pieces she asked her class to turn in weren't bad. Donnica could tell the ones who stayed were really serious about their work. She went through a few flash fiction exercise books and copied the ones she thought most useful. She'd only give them the ones she had done herself. Why teach them something she wasn't practicing?

Donnica got to the Y early that day. Careful not to spill her frozen coffee, she hurried past the desk. On her way to the stairs, she stopped once she saw Amber coming down them.

Donnica hadn't seen Amber since the day Point Set let her go. She looked around to see if she could find a way to avoid her. The way Amber was looking down as her feet hit each step gave her time, but this was the only way to Donnica's classroom.

Amber looked up and her eyes widened at Donnica's presence.

"Hi, Amber. What are you doing here?" Donnica asked, stepping closer to the wall to lean against the rail. She gripped her back with one hand and glanced at the cup in her other hand.

Amber's eyes shined a little as she looked towards the stairs behind her and pointed.

"I was…my daughter has dance class. Is this where your community service is?" Amber asked.

Donnica inhaled and perspired with embarrassment. She wasn't sure if Amber would know about her punishment, but she did.

"Yeah, look…I'm…that was bad."

"Donnica, we were close, and I hated doing that to you," Amber said, stepping close to Donnica and gently touching her shoulder. "I fought for you. I did, but I had to do my job."

"I know. I don't blame you," Donnica responded. "I have to go, but you do still have my number,"

Amber said, giving Donnica a knowing smile.

"Yes, I do." Donnica laughed as they passed each other.

While the class worked on a ten-minute writing exercise, Donnica couldn't help but think about her encounter with Amber. It was as if over the last month, Donnica had been masking her feelings with alcohol, and the glaze over her eyes was clearing up.

She felt disappointed in herself. Although she had been having fun preparing for this class, more than she anticipated, her personal writing was still suffering. No idea seemed to stick, and she had resorted to sending off old short stories to journals and literary magazines for a little income. She had pitched a few chapters of a book to several publishing companies, but waiting to hear back from them felt like a rejection already. She never thought she'd be back in the position of looking for support again. It was as if she had started all over.

"I don't deserve to be doing this," she mumbled, but someone heard her.

"You okay?" Karmi asked.

Donnica shook her head and stood up.

"You all can take a break on the exercise. I have something to say."

Donnica waited until they all put their pens down before she closed her eyes and took a deep breath.

"A couple of months ago, my publishing company dropped me because of my failed novels. They both sold less than 5,000 copies, and instead of seeing out my contract, they decided I was a liability. So, I proceeded to damage the CEO's car."

A few gasps and confused looks filled the room.

Donnica wasn't even sure why she was sharing this with them, but she continued.

"I was arrested and put into a holding cell until my lawyer made a deal where I walked away with a fine and community service duties. That's why I'm here."

"Why are you telling us this?" Karmi asked. "I'm not better than any of you," Donnica said, throwing her hands up. "My writing hasn't been at all worthy the last year, and I don't even know how to teach. All I can do is offer my advice and help you along the way, if you're really serious about this class. That's why I'm telling you this. If you are looking for some well-educated professor who criticizes everything you do just because they have a title on the best seller list, then that's not me either."

"Good," another person said, "Because that's not what we want."

Donnica smiled.

"Well, in that case, finish the exercise."

While everyone was leaving out the class, Donnica asked them to drop off their exercises with her first. She noticed

Karmi was lagging behind. Donnica watched her walk slowly up to the desk with her paper in hand.

"You're the only one reading these, right?" Karmi asked.

The question took Donnica by surprise. She sat up straight in the chair and nodded.

"Yes, of course."

"Good," Karmi said, giving a small smile before placing her paper on top of the stack, facing down.

Donnica tapped her foot along the inside of the desk before gathering her things and leaving the room behind her.

The true character of a woman lies in her mind. What she feels, believes, and wishes when no one else is around dictates her actions in public. The wounds that never got the proper care may be hidden away to an uncaring eye, but never doubt their existence; never doubt their power. With pasts already written in permanent ink, we fail to see that our future doesn't have to be printed with the same pen.

CHAPTER EIGHT

LANGSTON

Bang, bang, bang!

Langston jerked out of his sleep as his eyes popped open and his brain rattled in his head.

"Langston, wake up!" Jessie yelled from outside his bedroom window.

He squinted to see her silhouette behind the blinds. "It's hot!" she whined.

Langston yelled back that he was up and instantly regretted it once his hangover headache intensified. He pushed himself off the bed and dragged his feet through his home until he reached the front door. Kayla hopped in with her backpack swinging from her shoulder. Langston smiled at his sister who sauntered in with Ashton on her hip. This was the third weekend Jessie had kept Kayla, but this time, she offered. Langston wouldn't deprive his family of spending time with his daughter, just as Jus told him not to deprive himself of fun.

His eyelids burned as he lay back on his couch and closed his eyes. He felt a weight on his stomach and smiled once he saw Ashton sitting up.

"Long night?" Jessie asked, standing over them. He nodded. "I'll make you some coffee."

When Jessie walked out of the room, Langston held onto Ashton so he wouldn't fall over. He could hear Kayla moving around in her room and hoped she would take an early nap. He struggled to keep Ashton on the couch with him until Jessie came back.

"Do you want me to take Kay to Mom's until you feel better?" Jessie asked.

"No."

Silence fell on the siblings as Langston downed the coffee and a bottle of water. Kayla occupied herself in her room, and when Jessie had stayed long enough for Ashton to fall asleep, Langston knew something was on her mind.

"What's up?"

"Just wanted to talk."

"About what?"

"When is the custody hearing?"

"October twenty-first."

"That's pretty soon!" Jessie said.

"Nothing's changing, Jessie." "You aren't nervous or worried?"

"Renee's a clown."

"She's still her mother, and most courts side with the mother," she stated, nodding.

Langston sat up and glared at her. "What's your point?"

"I just want you to be prepared."

He kept quiet, knowing she'd have more to say if he continued the conversation. It was disheartening to him that his family thought so little of what he was doing. He had been taking care of Kayla for the last two years. She was smarter than any kid in her daycare and would be attending preschool soon. He kept her clean, well fed, and happy.

Renee contributed to none of that. "When are you leaving?" he asked. "Dang, bro," Jessie said, laughing.

Langston shook his head. "No, I just promised Kay that I'd take her somewhere," he lied.

Jessie watched him for a second before shrugging her shoulders and walking into Kayla's room to get Ashton. Langston waited until Jessie left before going back into his room to lie down.

The rush of his hangover settled as he held his phone in the air to check his messages. He frowned as Alisha's name appeared in little caps, but smiled once the image of her red dress reappeared in his mind.

"I don't like to wait on men to call me," Alisha said. "Didn't know you were waiting," he replied. "I'll make it up to you."

"Yes, I'm sure," she said.

They both laughed.

"Did I catch you at a bad time?" Alisha asked. "I'm actually about to take my daughter to get some ice cream."

"Daughter?"

As soon as the word fell from Alisha's lips, Langston reminded himself that he hadn't told her about Kayla.

They only talked briefly on the phone before, and it was only once. Delving into each other's personal lives wasn't an option during their mutual flirting. He hadn't meant to conceal information, especially Kayla.

"Kayla. She's four."

"Well, she must be adorable."

Langston heard the words, but he also heard the disappointing undertone in it. He hadn't had many girlfriends since he and Renee split. In fact, besides rekindling a few old flames for physical pleasure, he hadn't had any. He found although most women claimed to love a man who took care of his responsibilities, no one wanted to play the mother role to Kayla, not even her own mother.

It made him sad for her. She did nothing wrong. She held unconditional love and innocence in her heart that Langston had never known before her birth. She could be mouthy at times, but she minded him when he told her to do things. She didn't ask for this, and as he stood at Kayla's doorway watching her attempt to make her bed, he became angry.

"Don't sound so disappointed next time," he told Alisha.

"Langston, I wasn't…I'm not." "Maybe we'll talk later."

Langston looked down at Kayla and asked if she needed help.

"Daddy, I got this," she said, rolling her eyes.

Langston smiled before leaning against her wall and crossing his arms over his chest. He watched her struggle for a second before telling her that if she admitted she needed his help, he'd take her for ice cream. She sighed and asked for him to help, and soon, they were on their way to Marble Slab.

Kayla liked sweet cream ice cream with a brownie mixed in. She always begged for a medium, but Langston always got her a small. As he sat and watched her eat it, his phone vibrated.

I'm sorry I was just shocked. I'd like to get to know you, if you'd let me.
-Alisha

Dinner would be nice? Tomorrow?
-Alisha

I'll see what I can do.
-L

The next day was routine for Langston and Kayla.

He'd get off work, get her from daycare, get them food, and then head to Renee's house. Kayla hadn't been feeling well, but since his mom wasn't available to watch her while he was at work, all he could do was give her some medicine and send her to daycare. Once he picked her up, Kayla complained about being hungry since she slept through snack time, so he took her to get some soup.

When they arrived at Renee's apartment, she was standing outside on the phone.

"Hey, Mini-me," she said, cradling her phone between her shoulder and ear while bending down to pick Kayla up. Kayla, who was too tired to resist, laid her head on Renee's shoulder. Renee smiled before kicking the door open and following behind Langston.

"I got her soup because her stomach's upset," Langston said.

"Mini-Me's tummy hurts?" Renee said, rubbing Kayla's belly.

Kayla rolled her eyes a little, and Langston tried not to laugh. On his way to the kitchen, he got a text from Alisha asking what time he would be picking her up.

He silently cursed, having forgotten all about his date with Alisha. He hadn't even tried to find a babysitter, and he was supposed to meet her in a few hours. His nose flared as he grabbed a spoon from the drawer and went back into the living room.

"Is this sandwich mine?" Renee asked, peeking in the bag.

Langston nodded before handing Kayla the spoon and sitting down across from them.

"What you doing tonight?" Langston asked.

"Nothing. I work in the morning. Why, what's up?"

"I need you to watch Kay for a couple of hours."

Renee looked up from her sandwich and eyed Langston. "I just told you that I have to work in the morning."

"I do, too. I'll be to get her by nine or so."

Renee shook her head. "I need sleep. I have to be at work at nine, and you know she never sleeps over here."

"That's because you don't make her lay down! All I'm asking for is a few hours. Damn, Renee, it's almost six now!"

"Don't yell at me. I said no. Maybe on a day when I'm off."

"Why the hell do I even keep bringing her over here? Why don't you just sign your rights over now? You ain't ever been a mother!"

"Langston, that's not fair!"

He jumped out of his seat. Renee sat back quickly, and Kayla began to cry. His face softened as he grabbed her and hugged her. Kayla threw her arms around his neck and buried her face into his chest, while Renee sat on the couch quietly.

"I'm sorry for yelling, Kay." "I wanna go home," she said. "That's where we're going."

Renee tried to call out to him as he snatched Kayla's bag off the couch and walked out without shutting the front door. Once he got Kayla in her car seat and started the engine, he pulled his phone out and sighed.

> *Sorry, can't make it. Don't want to worry you with my*
> *problems.*
> *-L*

By the time he'd gotten home, Kayla was sleep and he was ashamed. He'd never yelled in front of her like that. He shouldn't have let Renee get him that upset. He should have known she would say no. He moved careful, not to wake

Kayla, and made it all the way to her bed. When he walked into the living room, his phone beeped.

Well, maybe I can come see you and you can tell me about it.
-Alisha

Supporting roles in the story of your life are more important than they may seem. When someone you want to be involved doesn't come alive on the page, it can cause you to rethink the whole plot. Some characters in our lives are interchangeable, while others we cannot do without.

CHAPTER NINE

KARMI

*Made with a sea of unrighteous roots Tapping into the
unforgiveness of betrayal, an unrelenting hurt from one who
doesn't remember even planting the seed
The trees and foliage around her do not comprehend her
insecurity,
wondering how the stark unique beauty could feel so ugly
inside
How could this beauty of nature have an
un- quenching thirst for a cleanliness so long forgotten?
The failing run to fight the dryness left by that tainted bed of
leaves?
Those tall woods around her with aging oaks and faltering
positions swayed away from the outer finesse she held.
Their scars visible on their trunks to be ridiculed and
inspected
Those around her could never escape their indiscretions
Their inner turmoil causing outward pain She failed in her
attempts for empathy
Surely if they looked closer, a little deeper...they could see*

"Mommy…"

"And this color is just all wrong for the drapes I had in mind. It's like the woman at the fabric store didn't even hear me," Neiva said.

"Mommy, I need to tell you something." "What is it, Karmiti?"

Dr. Reynolds said it was time to tell her mother. Once she revealed her molester was a family friend, Dr. Reynolds said it was a step needed in her healing process.

"I, um…I'm going to get some ice cream before I come over," Karmi said. "Do you want some?"

"Child!" Neiva said, giggling. "No, but I'll see you soon."

Karmi stomped her foot in self-irritation before walking into the ice cream parlor. She stood in line behind a man and a little girl, and as she narrowed her eyes, she realized it was the guy from her writing class.

"Hey. Langston, right?" she asked.

Both the girl and the man turned around. "Yeah. Karmi?"

"Yep," she said, before looking down at the little girl. "She is too adorable."

"Thank you. I'm Kayla!" she said.

Langston rolled his eyes and Karmi laughed. "Nice to meet you, Kayla."

Langston stepped up to order for them, and Kayla called out her order. Karmi beamed.

"I get sweet cream ice cream with a brownie, too!"

Kayla smiled, showing all her little teeth before turning to Langston.

"Daddy, can she sit with us? I like her!"

Karmi's eyes bugged as she looked up at Langston and stood back a little.

"I'm sorry. I don't want to impose."

"No, it's fine," Langston said. "Gotta give the princess

what she wants. Unless you were getting yours to go?"

"No, I can stay and eat."

"So how do you like the class?" Langston asked. "More than I thought actually," Karmi said. She watched how Kayla tried to sneak her spoon into Langston's small cup, but he gently pushed it away. She laughed. "You are so cute."

"She hears that enough."

"She couldn't possibly," Karmi said.

"Can I call you Kar, like my dad calls me Kay?" "You sure can!"

"How old are you?" Langston asked. "Acting young, huh? I'm twenty-one." "You seem younger."

"Thanks," Karmi said. "How old are you?" "Twenty-six."

"You don't act so old," Karmi said.

Langston laughed. "Twenty-six is old?" "Old enough."

Karmi and Kayla got into a conversation about Dora and even got Langston involved. She ended up talking with them for almost an hour before she realized her mom was probably waiting on her. She told Langston she would see him in class and said bye to Kayla.

Karmi hated Friday nights at the galleria. There were so many teenagers running in and out of the department store. She huffed as she went to a table of polo shirts in the junior section and refolded them for the fifth time that evening. A co-worker walked past and knocked one off the table. Karmi picked it up and threw it at her.

They both laughed.

"This is torture," Karmi expressed.

Her co-worker agreed before walking away, leaving Karmi to move through the tables and racks re- straightening jeans and dresses. She glanced at her phone on her waist clip. Only an hour and a half left. It was Friday night, and she wanted to go home and write.

Ever since last week's class when Donnica revealed why she was teaching the class, Karmi had been writing every night. She had a notebook that she secretly vowed no one would ever read and pushed her frustration into it.

Whenever the low hum pulsated through her lower abdomen that usually led her into the next man's arms, she grabbed the notebook and the blanket and wrote for hours.

She hadn't ventured into writing anything other than her issue at hand. Dr. Reynolds had to know this had become her only alternative to sex. She wrote the hum away.

Karmi banged into a display near the fine jewelry counter, almost knocking it over. She gripped the silver border so it wouldn't fall over as her knee muscle tightened and a sharp pain thumped through her leg. She placed her forehead against the display and closed her eyes.

Karmi silently cursed as she limped back into the break room. She tried to bend her leg and ease the pain, shaking her hands violently in front of her to point the pain in another direction. When that didn't work, Karmi clocked out thirty minutes early.

As she slowly walked out of the department store, Karmi remembered she had parked near the food court in an attempt to get a small amount of cardio in. Her nose flared, and she pulled on a handful of her curls as she walked through the mall.

She was almost past the restaurants in the food court, when a laugh rose above the chatter and froze her where she stood.

Karmi hadn't heard it in nearly a decade. It still made her insides churn and her knees buckle. She stood in the middle of the food court, one arm suspended with her hand still gripping her hair.

It was as if she had stumbled into her parents' bedroom as a child while they were having sex. She didn't want to look, but her head began turning to the left anyway. Her mouth closed, and she inhaled sharply as her shoulders tensed. His dark hair was salted now with white streaks, but still with a neat braid down his back. He was lean, but his shoulders were still brawny. From his side profile, his short beard matched his hair. His eyes were low and narrow.

Hassun.

Karmi's mind screamed "RUN", but another voice told her to stay. She wanted him to notice her, to know he had broken her, to see what he had left.

However, when he glanced her way, it was only a stranger's second. He turned back to his company. Karmi's eyes burned to see a young girl hugging his waist.

He hadn't remembered her. The man who ignited an unwanted desire in her had forgotten her.

Who was the girl? His daughter? His latest victim? Had she been his doorway into a perverted life? Was she even the first?

As if being pushed, Karmi's feet finally moved and she barged out of the double doors, limping towards her car.

After locking herself inside, she pulled her phone out and fumbled with it to make a call.

"Can you meet me somewhere?"

Karmi bit her lip as she bent her leg to pull her leggings down in the back seat of the green Ford Escape. Her stomach tightened at the naked sight of Hush Nightclub, whose name she just learned was Khalil.

He gripped her hips and greedily pulled her into his lap.

She giggled out of instinct, swinging her right hand around to move her curls from her face.

The immediacy of her want died, but the hum was still there. She looked up at the roof of the car and tried to drown it out as she rocked in Khalil's lap.

He said something, but Karmi ignored him, just as she ignored the ring attached to the hand that handled her right breast. It was all irrelevant.

Karmi bit her lip harder, hoping the buzz in her head would overcome the hum in her body. She pulled Khalil closer, and after a few minutes, she finally felt what she wanted.

Nothing.

Karmi tried to erase her problems with Khalil again the next night. She had been roaming around Hermann Park near Rice University for a few hours. Karmi watched the mini red train carry small children and their parents through the park over the metal path of the tracks. She could hear them laughing and eagerly pointing things out to their mothers and fathers, who nodded and smiled down at them. The small huff of the train passed her before she aimlessly wandered into the Japanese Garden near Sam Houston's monument.

She remembered the stories throughout school of the great commander-in-chief and how he was no respecter of persons, some of his best friends being Native Americans. Karmi always thought her teachers were just trying to make her feel better about being a minority. Karmi resented them for it.

But, the Japanese Garden was one of her favorite things about the park. The calming sounds of the small waterfall and the rounded greens of the multiple bushes relaxed her.

Karmi took a seat on one of the gray concrete benches near the teahouse and straightened her back as she inhaled. She thought of the past six years of her life and how there wasn't a day when Karmi was not haunted by thoughts of Hassun. Something inside of her twisted and churned at not even being a memory he couldn't escape. She thought possibly he was ignoring her, not wanting to acknowledge her, but then there would have been some type of stare or glance that gave him away.

Her neck tightened and heat flushed her skin as she moved her head side to side to release some of the pressure. The heel of her shoe tapped against the path just as her phone vibrated in her purse.

Turned out that Khalil and his wife's apartment wasn't too far from the park, and the latter was currently out shopping. Everything in her right mind was telling her to decline his offer to stop by. Karmi didn't want to be that woman, even if she had already slept with him. The hum inside of her didn't allow her to turn him down, though.

Khalil's apartment was quiet despite the noise coming from their union. Karmi made it no further than the living room, not having the heart to venture into the marital bedroom. The couch was just as sinful because the two were so wrapped up in their dance of passion that neither of them heard the keys turning inside the lock. His wife's voice rang out in a mixture of anger and disappointment.

Before Karmi could react, she was being pulled off of the couch and Khalil's lap by a fistful of her hair.

While Karmi scrambled to get her footing to defend herself, his wife screamed that she knew she would catch him. Khalil struggled to pull his sweats up as his wife swung her fist into Karmi's eyes repeatedly until he was able to hold her off. They fell to the floor, his wife on top of him as he held her tightly in his arms. She kicked and screamed for him to let her go as he yelled for Karmi to leave.

Karmi scrambled to pull her dress down and then grabbed her underwear, sandals, and purse before rushing to the door. She ran all the way to her car and locked herself inside.

The excruciating pain in her eye thumped as she cried hard into the steering wheel. Her body shook with shame, and she cried harder because she had no idea how to stop the feeling.

Tears mixed with her saliva as she opened her mouth and cried, while looking up at the ceiling of her car and shaking her head. This was a pain she had no idea how to cope with. So, Karmi cried until she couldn't anymore.

CHAPTER TEN

DONNICA

Pappasito's Catina was buzzing from the lunchtime rush, with the aromas of authentic Mexican dishes passing Donnica and Amber's table every few minutes.

The round wooden table wobbled slightly as Donnica rested her elbows on it, her chin in the palm of her hand. She blinked slowly before narrowing her eyes on Amber's hair.

"Can you stop staring like that?" Amber said, tilting her head to the left, making her newly shortened tresses sway.

Donnica smiled, showing all her teeth. "I just never imagined you with different hair. The black is really cute, but the cut threw me off."

"I know, but changes needed to be made," Amber said, running her hand over her hair.

Donnica looked down at her ring finger and missed her wedding ring. She just didn't feel right wearing it when things with Jeremiah weren't great.

"So what's up?"

"Funny thing," Amber said. "I was reviewing this new author that the Big Boys are pushing hard and the storyline was horrible. It had no depth to it. She was like a porn writer that they were trying to push off as mysterious romance. I hated it."

Donnica laughed at how animated Amber was being. She was waving her arms and making faces as if she were disgusted. Their food came while Amber was giving Donnica the rundown on the direction Point Set was going in.

"And no offense to you, but they were describing projects that were like *Burning Desires*."

"I've put it behind me."

"D, I felt like I was going to burst in that meeting. I had to do something."

"What did you do?" Donnica asked, while looking down at the ingredients for her chicken fajitas. She inhaled the grilled goodness and jiggled a little in her seat.

"I quit."

Donnica looked up at Amber and studied her face. Her lips were stone as she looked up at Donnica before a smile slowly spread across her face.

"You are not serious."

"I put in my resignation a few days ago, and it feels better than I thought."

"What are you going to do now?" "I have a few things in mind."

"What do you have up your sleeve, girl?"

Amber didn't reply. She just picked up her burrito and bit into it. With small pieces of the tortilla peaking out of her teeth, she smiled at Donnica and they both laughed.

"You are hilarious."

"You don't have many friends, do you?" Amber joked, but Donnica shook her head.

"I'm more of a loner."

"Good thing," Amber said. "We wouldn't get any work done."

Donnica read over the poem twice before putting it down on her desk. After a few other poems, Donnica went back to

Karmi's. She hadn't read a poem that was so clear to her in a while, and it was definitely refreshing. She closed her eyes as she envisioned the scene. Karmi was wonderful at imagery, but Donnica hadn't really paid attention to it until she read the poem.

Donnica's curiosity about Karmi heightened at the possible truth in her art. She didn't want to dig into Karmi's life, especially since she looked like the type who wouldn't appreciate that. However, Donnica felt an urge to help her. How? She didn't know.

It had been two months since the class started, and Donnica was humbled. It had been awhile since she'd been in a workshop atmosphere. She wasn't used to people giving her critical feedback that she didn't like but was needed. The people around her were not praising her accomplishments or even picking at her failures. She didn't know how it happened this way, but Donnica was ready to start another project with her new mindset, hoping something would come out great enough to save her career.

But, first, she needed Jeremiah.

After countless phone calls and surprise visits, Jeremiah agreed to have dinner with her. Instead of going to a restaurant, Donnica decided to try one of the oldest tricks in the book; cooking Jeremiah's favorite meal.

She cleaned the house and made sure her appearance was worthy of forgiveness. After coming home from the grocery store, Donnica began to get nervous. She was stepping out on faith and prayed she was wrong about being convinced almost a year ago that her marriage was over. She hoped he would still want to work it out. She didn't know if he was still dating or if he had gotten serious with someone; Donnica definitely didn't want that.

So, she prepped her dinner of T-bone steaks with sautéed mushrooms and onions, baked sweet potatoes, and asparagus with cheese before going into her office to reread her students' work.

It had taken some time not to rely on wine to soothe her since Point Set let her go. Donnica knew if she hadn't found a solace in teaching this class, she wouldn't have. Part of her still felt numb, though, and that was only a part that Jeremiah could bring feeling back to.

When she heard the lock on the front door click and a few buttons pushed on the alarm, she smiled. Jeremiah had used his key like she had asked. Donnica decided against rushing to greet him. Instead, she sat up in the chair, leaning over the arm and crossing her legs towards the way she leaned. She tapped her foot against the desk and waited to hear his footsteps. He always knew where to find her.

He turned the corner into her office with a knowing smile, and she returned it. She loved his new casual attitude that came out through his appearance. He was still neat and clean, but him wearing a suit every day always bothered Donnica. She felt like he never actually relaxed. Jeremiah wore a pair of shorts and a short-sleeve button down with those leather sandals that guys wore.

"Should have known you'd be stashed away in here," he said.

Donnica stood up and wrapped her arms around his neck, hugging him tightly.

"Had some papers to look over, but dinner is almost ready."

She pulled back, but he held her at arm's length. "I like this dress."

She blushed before Jeremiah let her go. She had on a simple red and gray striped cotton dress that fit comfortably to her curves. She hated wearing shoes in the house, so she opted for a nice pedicure instead.

Donnica walked around him into the kitchen to check the food.

Dinner was seamless. Jeremiah was more talkative than he had been with her in some months. Donnica almost didn't have to say anything. She noticed his new cool demeanor with every word and thrived on it. As she cleared their plates from the table, a sudden realization hit her.

Maybe Jeremiah's new attire and attitude were due to a new woman in his life.

Donnica's heart dropped as she finished off her glass of lemonade before making two bowls of black cherry ice cream and heading back to the living room where Jeremiah said he'd be.

"I put a little chocolate sauce on yours," Donnica mumbled, sitting on the other end of the couch and curling her feet under her legs.

Jeremiah commented on how much he loved the dessert mix, but Donnica just stared at the television.

She wanted to cry. She didn't know why Jeremiah hadn't gone through with the divorce yet since he was clearly involved with someone else. She couldn't even finish her ice cream.

"It's getting late."

"I wasn't planning on leaving yet. You want me to go?" Jeremiah asked, confused.

"You don't have to stay with me any longer." "Tonight?" Donnica didn't reply. "What's the problem, D? You just switched up on me within minutes."

"You don't have to pretend like you aren't involved with someone," Donnica said, not being able to hold her emotions. "I know."

"You know what? That you're completely delusional?" he asked, laughing.

Donnica's nose flared. "Don't patronize me!" "Donnica, I am not involved with someone else. I went on a few dates, but that was it."

Donnica's head fell as she closed her eyes and prayed it was true. She needed her husband. The weight on the couch shifted, and Jeremiah's body heat radiated to hers.

"I was actually hoping I could stay tonight," he spoke, his bravado just above a whisper. "I wanted to sleep next to my wife and talk about what that means in the morning."

Donnica's back lifted from the couch as Jeremiah wrapped his arms around her and pulled her into his chest, chuckling when she didn't resist.

Donnica sat behind her desk with her legs crossed, tilting her legs side to side while biting her lip and holding her phone up to her ear.

"Come back when you leave there."

"Jay, I haven't been home in two days," Donnica said. "You know you're coming," he said, and she smiled.

Ever since their dinner, they hadn't spent a day apart from each other unless Jeremiah had to work. It felt nice to have his companionship again. Donnica had to admit she was glad they were taking it slow, though.

She looked up to see Karmi coming into the room with streaks of mascara down her cheeks. Karmi stopped in the doorway and tried to wipe it off.

"I'll be over later," Donnica said, getting off the phone with Jeremiah. "Karmi, are you okay?"

Saying nothing, Karmi walked through the rows of desks

before taking a seat in one directly in front of Donnica. They stared at each other before Donnica pulled out a small pack of tissue and stood up. Once she got closer to Karmi, Donnica could see the red bruise under her eye. Donnica frowned.

"Do you want to talk about it?"

Karmi shook her head. Donnica sighed before sitting on the edge of her own desk. Karmi's curls were pushed back from her face with a green headband and a pair of sunglasses. She glared at Donnica for so long that

Donnica moved around the desk to her stack of papers. She sifted through them and came upon Karmi's name.

"Here's your poem," she said. "I hope you don't mind that I made a copy."

"Why would you do that?" Karmi asked.

"I've never read a poem like this before," Donnica told her, sitting in the desk next to Karmi.

"Yeah, right," Karmi said. She started to laugh but stopped because of Donnica's expression. "Are you serious?"

"I don't play when it comes to good writing," Donnica replied. "Karmi, you're good. Most of the class is good, but you are really good."

"I didn't know," she mumbled. "It's fictional, right?"

Karmi didn't respond. Donnica frowned before putting her hand over her mouth.

"I'm sorry. I thought…"

"I don't want to talk about it."

"You don't have to," Donnica said, Karmi looking up at her. Donnica placed her hand on top of Karmi's paper. "Let this talk for you."

The rest of the class soon filed in the room, and Donnica began the night's lesson. After her conversation with Amber earlier in the week, she knew there was a need for good literature in Houston, especially in the fiction genre. Best sellers had become cliché, and it was time for a change. Even if it was only a little change, Donnica wanted to be a part of it.

"Before you all go, I have something to run past you," Donnica said.

"Another exercise?" Langston asked.

The rest of the class laughed.

"No. This is about the end of class," Donnica said, somehow just now feeling that the three months had gone by quickly. "We only have a few weeks left, and you all have progressed so well. What better way to showcase that to your family and friends than a literary reading?"

Donnica smiled as the class began to murmur amongst each other.

While reading into someone else's truth, we sometimes realize that our own story is not that bad. Delving into their past can lead us to interesting revelations not only about that person, but about ourselves. It causes us to be grateful for our own fates. Then we realize the problems that we thought were unfixable in our lives really aren't that bad.

CHAPTER ELEVEN

LANGSTON

"My poem was definitely better than yours."

"Cocky much?"

Langston propped his leg up on the couch as Karmi laughed. They had been on the phone for about an hour. Kayla had decided that before going to sleep she needed to talk to Karmi or she'd cry herself to sleep. With the impending drama of tomorrow, he wasn't in the mood to test her.

Kayla ended up sleep and Langston continued the conversation. He found out that he liked talking to her. She was smart for her age and not as quiet as she seemed.

Langston anticipated her quirky remarks.

"Donnica said I should try to publish it. It's just a little too personal."

"Are you going to let me read it?"

"No," Karmi responded quickly. "Not the poetry."

Langston wanted to ask her why, just as he had wanted to ask her about the black eye forming that he noticed in class a few days before. He hadn't known her long, but Langston knew Karmi was a very private person.

Something in her life was causing her pain, something so great that it made little joys like sharing the same favorite ice cream as a four-year-old significant.

He didn't want her to be uncomfortable with him, so he didn't delve into her personal life.

"Kay says she wants you to see her Dora bed." "Awww, she is the cutest!" Karmi said, almost yelling.

Langston shook his head. "She's okay," he joked.

"I would say I wish I had one, but, nope, not now."

He laughed and asked her if she ever did. Karmi replied she might one day, that she'd have to get over some things first.

Langston yawned as he checked on Kayla, who had fallen asleep in the middle of his bed. He decided to leave her there and slid into the bed next to her. The pillow-top mattress puffed and raised Kayla's body as it sunk under him. The coolness of the sheets relaxed him.

Spending weekends partying had nothing on moments like these. He smiled at her mouth being open and the light snores coming out. He gently poked her nose, and she frowned before turning the other way.

Langston may have been annoyed by responsibility, but he needed Kayla with him. He didn't want Renee to have that joy.

But, the next day, the judge decided Renee deserved it with an order for joint custody. He watched Renee and her sister celebrate on the other side of the room as his lawyer patted his shoulder and walked away. He wondered why she was so happy. He had been the one to file for custody.

Jus, who greeted him outside the courtroom, tried to make light of the situation by saying joint was better than none, but Langston was numb.

He tried to make it out of the building without speaking with Renee, but she caught him at the door.

"I'm off Friday. I'll pick her up then."

Langston glared at her from head to toe before trying to walk away from her. She grabbed his arm.

"Don't be like this, Langston. I'm doing this for us."

"What are you talking about?"

"I know you left because I wasn't being a great mother, but I'm trying now. Joint custody was the best thing for both of us until we can work on being a family again."

Langston watched her lips move and wished those words would have been spoken two years ago when they would've meant something. His heart pounded in his ears, drowning out her voice. His face was stone as he stepped closer to Renee and Justin tried to pull him back.

"You are out of your damn mind. I don't trust you with my kid. She doesn't even like to be around you. You think I still want you?"

"Langston," Renee interjected, her eyes now glossy.

"You could have talked to me about this! You could have seen her more through me! You didn't even want her!"

Jus began to pull Langston out the door as his voice grew louder. Langston fought against him, but Jus pinned him to his truck.

"Bro, calm down! This is not the place!"

"She really did this? She doesn't even want her, Jus!" "You can appeal it."

"On paper she's a good mother." "Don't some courts let the kid speak?"

"I'm not putting Kay through that," Langston said, hanging his head.

The drive to Renee's house had been heartbreaking. Langston called off work the last few days to spend more time with Kayla. He had made it a regular routine to take her to Renee's after daycare each day, but this day, he would be leaving without her.

The hum of his car's engine filled the silence as he sat in traffic, thankful for it that day.

"Daddy, play my song," Kayla whined from the backseat.

"I don't have it right now." "Radio broke?"

"We're almost at Mommy's."

"Fine," Kayla said with an exasperated sigh. Langston smirked as traffic began to move. "You mad?" Kayla asked.

"No, baby. Why you ask me that?" "You got that look."

"You are way too smart for your own good." "Your fault."

Langston laughed this time, and Kayla smiled at him through the rearview, proud of her victory. He had been thinking of ways to let Kayla know that she would be spending the night with Renee. He didn't want to ambush her into the situation and make her feel as if he was abandoning her. She started singing some Kirk Franklin song that Langston's mother taught her. He prayed this didn't change her. He would be there as much as he could, but he knew if Renee was actually trying that he couldn't stand in the way. After all, she was Kayla's mother.

"You are having a sleepover with Renee tonight," Langston said, glancing at her to gauge her reaction.

Kayla shrugged her shoulders. "She snores."

Langston laughed and told her that she wouldn't have to sleep with Renee. In fact, Renee had turned her extra room into Kayla's room. She had bought her clothes and things as well, but Langston was still skeptical. After their little scene in court, he would be watching her hard. He didn't need Kayla to be just a pawn in Renee's scheme to get him back.

He had a date with Alisha later. Between her and Karmi, he felt better about the joint custody. He and Alisha were more intimate, and he decided that dating wouldn't be bad.

Karmi was the friend he needed. She moved into his life by way of Kayla, and although he was sure if Kayla hadn't fallen in love with her that their involvement outside of the creative class would be nonexistent, he was glad it happened. She was fun and honest—two things he could appreciate. Langston knew Karmi needed a friend, too, and he planned on being there for her whenever she was ready to open up about her problems.

She had done that for him.

Kayla unfastened her seatbelt, pulling it around her seat as Langston opened the back door and held his arms out. She clutched his shoulders as they made their way to Renee's.

She swung the door open and smiled, bouncing her weight from leg to leg. After she moved to let them in, Langston noticed the lemon smell and how clean the living room looked.

"Lemon bars?" Langston asked.

Renee nodded.

"Your mom's been here?"

"Yes, actually," Renee replied. "But, I made them." "Yeah, right," Langston said, laughing as he put Kayla down on her own two feet.

Renee rolled her eyes before jogging into the kitchen and coming back with a small golden bar in her hand. She pushed it into Langston's hand, and he tasted it.

"It's not as good as your moms, but you're close," he commented. Renee shrugged.

"Come on, I need your help," she said, pulling on his wrist and going down the hall.

She pushed the door to Kayla's new room open and pulled Langston inside.

No princess bed, he thought. Shaking his head, he looked around at the pink, grey, and red room, trying to find something else wrong.

"I feel like something's missing," Renee said, biting her lip. She pulled on her fingers with her left hand and looked around the room frantically. Langston looked her up and down before his shoulders relaxed. He stood next to her, examining the room as well.

"Dora," he said. "She won't sleep without a Dora comforter."

Renee looked up at him and smiled. "Dora it is."

You never realize how important you are to someone's story. Every relationship, those platonic friendships and intimate ones, grows in different ways. Whether you want to be a major character or not, your story often intertwines with theirs in ways you may not understand until you read it yourself.

CHAPTER TWELVE

KARMI

I imagine my big brother would find me quite annoying
I'd want to tag along with him and his friends, make him play
with my dolls and try to steal his clothes during my tomboy
phase
I'd hate all his girlfriends because they were occupying my
time
Hide his car keys when he became old enough to drive
I'd cry to Mom that he was too overprotective when I flirted
with his friends
Secretly, I'd love that he still cares.
I imagine my big brother would give the best pep talks
Cheering me on in victories and talking me out of my faults
He'd question all of my motives and always know when I lied
He'd be the only person to know I'm hurting but smiling on
the outside
I imagine him to be a jerk I imagine him to be wise
I imagine him to be hilarious, but only in my eyes
I imagine he'll tell me the truth, whether I like it or not
Now, I don't imagine everything that I've got

"Spring lamb soup?"

"It tastes a lot better than it sounds," Karmi said, laughing at Langston's expression.

The pair walked down the spice aisle in Town and Country Supermarket to get the ingredients Karmi needed for the soup. She hadn't seen her mother in a few days due to work, and missing her triggered a craving for a dish that flavored her childhood. She was away at a quilting convention, so Karmi hoped the soup would last until she got home.

She wanted to speak with her mother about Hassun, but after seeing him, she realized it was time she stopped blaming him for her wrong decisions. He had been a constant reminder of Karmi losing herself. He didn't remember that girl who he brainwashed and molested. He hadn't thought about how a confused adolescent could transfer those feelings of filth and confusion into comfort and stability. Why should she?

Langston had been bumming around on his day off, so he decided to accompany Karmi to the store and try the soup, too.

"It has actual lamb in it?"

Karmi's eyebrows came closer together as she glanced at Langston on the other side of the cart. His lips were perched as he examined the pack of meat in the bottom of the cart. Karmi smiled before laughing.

"If it's cooked right, it tastes like chicken. Stop being a baby."

"I'm not!" Langston said. "I just like to eat what I know."

"How do you live in Houston and not try different things to eat?" Karmi asked.

Langston shrugged. Karmi left the issue alone and picked up the spices she needed: garlic, coriander seed, and peppercorn. Only other ingredients she needed were a few onions and pinto beans.

"Are you excited about the reading?" Langston asked.

Karmi's chest swelled as she inhaled before smiling.

"I am actually. It feels good to be doing something productive."

"I still can't believe you won't let me read anything." "You'll have to wait like everyone else."

"You let Donnica read it," Langston teased.

"She's helping me, so that's different," Karmi said, before sticking her tongue out at him. "Why didn't you sign up, though?"

"I'm not that good at it," Langston admitted.

"Truthfully, I only did it because my lawyer thought it would look good."

"How are you holding up?" Karmi asked.

"It's not as bad as I thought. Renee is really trying, and Kayla is bonding with her a little more."

"That's good."

"I miss her like crazy on the days that she's away, but it's nice to have a little free time to do me, you know?"

Even though she didn't know, Karmi nodded, just happy that he had found the good in the joint custody requirement. She was never responsible for anyone except herself, and up until lately she hadn't been doing a great job with that.

"Well, since you're cooking dinner, I'll get dessert," Langston said.

"Ice cream?" Karmi asked with a smile. Langston nodded and smiled.

They joked around as they turned towards the freezer section. Langston's steps skipped a beat, and Karmi looked up from the cart to see why.

"Alisha?"

The taller woman looked up from reaching into one of coolers and smiled.

"Hey, baby," she said, walking away from her cart and into Langston's arms.

Karmi smiled at their public display of affection but wondered who she was. Langston gave the woman a quick kiss before pulling away.

"Lisha, this is the homie Karmi," Langston said.

Karmi had to laugh at his introduction. "Oh, hi," Alisha said.

Karmi could tell the woman was wondering if she was more than a friend. Karmi had been in that situation too many times not to recognize that look.

Her initial reaction was to quickly explain their relationship. She wouldn't want to bring any issues to Langston, who had been a great friend to her. She opened her mouth to speak but noticed Langston had already done so.

"She's about to cook me an authentic Native American dish, so call me later to make sure I'm alive."

Karmi's cheeks puffed as she laughed while bending over the cart. Langston smirked at his own joke as Alisha looked between the two, confused.

"Well, maybe we can meet up a little later?" she asked, running her hand down his arm.

Karmi tensed at the thought of Langston leaving. Of course, they were platonic friends, but he had promised her that evening.

She gently rubbed the irritating, yet healing bruise under her eye and tried not to panic. She was ashamed of it, and being in this situation with Langston oddly reminded her of the third time she had slept with Khalil, whom she reverted back to calling Hush Nightclub after finding out he was married.

The sex between them had gotten rough and sporadic, and one mistake of going back to his place had landed her with a black eye at the hands of his wife.

She gripped the cart and moved slightly back, looking for an escape route. Langston's hand at the end of the cart prohibited her.

"We actually had today planned, and I'm hoping Renee gets tired of Kay and brings her home today," Langston said.

Karmi frowned and looked at him. Did he just reject this woman he seemed to be intimate with? For her?

Karmi bit the inside of her lip as Langston kissed the woman again before pulling the cart and Karmi towards the checkout.

"Um, are you sure that was a good idea?" she asked.

Langston looked at her and frowned. "What? You trying to cancel on me?" he asked.

Karmi shook her head violently. "No. I just don't want to cause any problems."

"That's funny," Langston said. "Alisha and I are cool but we aren't that serious. Plus, I said I was chilling with my homie today, right? I didn't forget."

Karmi smiled.

No, she thought. *You didn't forget me.*

CHAPTER THIRTEEN

DONNICA

Donnica rushed down the corridor of the courthouse looking for room 254 while checking the time on her cell phone. She gripped the leather strap on her purse so it wouldn't slip off her shoulder as she hurried.

"Amber is going to kill me," she mumbled, stopping in front of her destination to catch her breath.

"She would if the lawyer's previous meeting hadn't run over," Amber said, coming out of the women's bathroom next door to the office.

Donnica rolled her eyes before placing both hands on the knees of her black slacks and catching her breath.

"You are always late." Amber laughed.

"Sorry," Donnica said, holding one hand up. "Had a few last minute promos for the reading." "Sounding like a good turnout?" Amber asked.

They both sat down on the wooden bench outside the door.

"It's promising. Are you coming?" Donnica inquired. "With a date!"

"How do you bring a date to a literary reading?" Donnica asked.

Amber glanced at her and frowned, turning her shoulders slightly. "Easy."

Donnica shook her head before pulling a manila folder out of her purse and handing it to Amber. The two couldn't help but smile as Amber bounced around in her seat.

"Everything's good on my end," Donnica said. "Jeremiah had a meeting with the senior partners, but if he's needed, he'll be here."

"This should be quick. I can't believe it's so quick!"

"This is when the hard work starts," Donnica said.

Amber glanced at her with a tight smile. "You up for it?"

Donnica looked at her and smiled.

Amber was starting her own publishing company and wanted Donnica to help her manage it. She was never sure if her heart was in it, but since her own writing hadn't been the best lately, she figured she could still identify what the best was. She would be in charge of recruiting writers until bigger dreams materialized and they would need more hands.

Jeremiah thought it was a great idea. It would help Donnica find her inspiration again while still working in the literary world. She and Amber had always been connected through words, a winning situation for them both.

"Ladies, Mr. Kyle says come on in," his secretary said as she opened the door and turned to greet them.

Amber stood out and held her arm to Donnica, bent at the elbow as an escort. Donnica stood and looped her arm with Amber's.

"Yeah, I think I'm up for it."

With all of the financials, marketing, and planning out the way, it was now the last day of Donnica's class and the night of the reading. Ron had let Donnica's class set up in the upstairs gym, and Donnica called in a favor from

Jeremiah's cousin to have it set up like an open mic night at a jazz club.

The lights were dim and round tables were scattered around the small stage up against the main wall. If it weren't for the bleachers, it could pass.

She had her readers at a separate table as people began to file in. Karmi, along with a few other classmates, had signed up, and Donnica even had a few sign up through her social networking page online. She had six readers total, which was a good number so each of them could read a few of their poems.

As each one stood and read their work, Donnica examined the faces in the crowd. She could easily make out the others from class who didn't want to speak sitting in the front. Amber, her date, and Jeremiah were seated near them. Jeremiah winked at her, and Amber smiled while crossing her fingers in the air. Donnica smiled back and clapped once the host called Karmi's name.

She wanted Karmi to go last.

Her poetry held such emotion that Donnica wanted everyone to be in the spirit of poetry before she got up. Donnica waved to get Amber's attention as Karmi prepared herself at the stand.

"She's the one?" Amber mouthed.

Donnica nodded, and Amber turned in her chair to give her full attention to Karmi. After their meeting with the lawyer, Donnica couldn't praise Karmi's work enough. Amber always wanted to do a poetry anthology, and Donnica thought Karmi would be the perfect feature.

New talent was always refreshing to Donnica, especially when it was a raw gift that didn't need much revision.

But that's what life is, Donnica thought.

She remembered the old phrase used in all of her creative writing classes: *writing is rewriting*. She had rewritten her current situation without even knowing it. New business ventures with a true friend had allowed her to see her visions in new ways that helped her amend her whole life.

Revisions used to be Donnica's nemesis, but the healing power it had couldn't go unnoticed any longer.

The words of another can be so inspiring in your life that they lead you to open up new pages in your own journey. You may not know the extent of that person's pain, but through their words you realize you've been connected to them through a creative bond that can only strengthen all of those involved. Do not be afraid to be inspired.

CHAPTER FOURTEEN

LANGSTON

Langston eyed his younger brother as he plopped down on his couch. Using each foot to remove the sneaker on the other foot, Jus sighed as each shoe hit the carpet with a soft thud. He stretched out, folding his arms behind his head, and closed his eyes.

"And you're here this early because?" Langston asked. "I told you, my stalker is off work. She knows where I live."

Langston shook his head.

"Well, I was going to take Kayla to Mom's for a minute, but since you're here, you can watch her while I run."

"She's still sleep?"

Langston nodded just as someone knocked on his door. While Jus only glanced towards the door, Langston got up and answered it.

Karmi walked in with her yoga gear on ready to go. It was a black and orange Capri pants set with a sleeveless matching tank. Her curls were pulled into a tight ninja bun on top of her head.

"Let's get this over with," she said dryly.

Langston laughed at her as Karmi noticed Jus on the couch. Jus sat up and looked at her.

"Karmi, my brother Justin. Jus, Karmi was in that writing class at the Y."

Jus nodded as Karmi waved before greeting him. Jus squinted a little before he smiled and returned her salutation. Karmi shifted uncomfortably in her spot by the door. Langston frowned.

"No more than an hour," he said.

Jus waved Langston off while getting back into his position on the couch and closing his eyes. Langston stepped out of the front door after Karmi. She placed her hands on her hip before stretching side to side and then bending down to touch her toes. She looked up once Langston laughed.

"What?"

"We just running two miles," he said, still laughing, then jogged off towards the sidewalk.

"Oh, whatever, old man!" Karmi said, catching up with him.

The smooth pave on the sidewalks of his neighborhood radiated heat as the two jogged down them. Rounded corners and the small dips of driveways added a little texture to their run. Langston had been trying a lot of different things to fill his free time now. It was as good a time as any to get back in shape.

Karmi stayed ahead of him for most of the first run. Her path wasn't straight; her stride went from side to side, so Langston kept a few feet behind her to avoid any collisions. They stopped at the dead end near a small playground for a few minutes. With her hair pinned up, Langston could see a small cut running the length of her ear. The skin around it was chapped, and although her black eye was gone, he figured they both happened the same day.

"You ever going to tell me what happened to your eye?"

Karmi's body stiffened before she exhaled. "Why does it matter?"

"I don't know," Langston said. "Maybe I'm just trying to make sure you aren't stuck in any crazy situations."

He watched her look up at the sun and squint before sucking her teeth.

"No, definitely not in any of those."

"Well, let's finish this run."

Karmi took off first and Langston followed.

"What's the chick's name again?"

Langston downed a bottle of water while watching Jus post up against his kitchen counter. He kicked his feet out a little before crossing his arms and giving his big brother his attention.

"Karmi."

Jus looked towards the ceiling and bit the inside of his lip before nodding. "I've seen her before," he said.

Langston turned his body towards Jus and watched his face light up with acknowledgement.

"She was more done up, but I definitely remember her."

Langston eyed his brother after noticing the tone his voice began to take. Langston wasn't sure why he was so concerned about the innuendo in what Jus was saying.

"How do you know her?"

"I've seen her a couple of times with my boy."

"With your boy?"

"A few times," Jus said, smiling. "We've talked about her."

"Say what you're saying and get it over with," Langston said, feeling his face get hot.

Jus laughed before shaking his head. Just then, Kayla came skipping around the corner and stole Langston's attention.

"Did you run fast?" she asked.

"Fast enough," Langston replied, before handing her a pack of fruit snacks.

She grinned before running back into her room. "Be careful with her," Jus said.

"Kayla?"

"No, Karmi."

"We're just cool. She's a little young anyway."

"And a little loose," Jus commented.

Langston looked up at him and frowned.

"She's been with a few guys from the club scene," Jus added.

"That doesn't mean much."

"Yeah, okay," Jus said. "I'm out."

Langston heard Jus tell Kayla bye before he left.

Langston stood there for a moment before going to clean up from his run. Just as Langston got out of the shower, his cell phone rang. It was Alisha.

"Hey, stranger."

"What's up?"

"Finally off of work, wanting to see if you were busy tonight."

"You had plans?" Langston asked with a smile as he walked through his home, checking to see which room Kayla was in. She had gotten quiet, and he wanted to make sure she wasn't doing anything sneaky.

"Thought we could catch a movie or a late dinner," Alisha suggested.

Something about her tone let Langston know she was biting her lip or smiling. He found Kayla in the corner of her room at her small table, coloring a large rabbit in with a green crayon. He sat on her bed and watched her.

"I got my little one this weekend," Langston said, finally

realizing he hadn't answered her. "Sorry, sweetie."

Alisha sighed. Langston expected whining or some type of attitude to follow, but all he heard was her hum.

"Maybe I can come over?" Alisha asked and then it was Langston's turn to sigh.

"I don't know."

"Why not?" Alisha asked, finally whining. "We've been dating for a little while now. You know I'm a good person. Why can't I meet her?"

Langston watched Kayla hold the picture up to him with an eye for approval. After he nodded, she smiled before flipping the page to the next blank picture that awaited her colors.

"Alisha, I know you're a good person. I'm just careful with who I bring around her."

Alisha mumbled something, but the background noise of her car stereo kept Langston from comprehending.

"What did you say?" "Nothing."

"Is there a problem?"

"I'm saying, Langston, you let that girl around Kayla, and she's not a great role model for little girls at all."

"What are you talking about?"

"You know who I'm talking about!"

"Why is everyone so worried about Karmi?" Langston asked, getting up and walking out of Kayla's room. "We're just friends."

"So Justin told you and you still let her come around?" Alisha asked.

"She's done nothing wrong to me or my child." "And I haven't either."

"This is stupid. If it means so much to you, just come over," Langston said.

Alisha was quiet for a while before she spoke again. "No, thanks. I don't want to anymore."

Langston began to worry about Karmi. He had known she had issues, but with both his brother and Alisha bringing it up, he wasn't sure if she was someone he wanted around his daughter. He had trusted her up until now, but his brother was right; he had to be careful. He had to get some answers.

You can never truly know a person's whole story until you read it for yourself. The first few chapters can give you an idea of their inner being. Yet, assuming what's to come based off of what you read is not an intelligent thing to do. Always be careful and pay attention. However, judging the book without reading to the end can be detrimental, as well.

CHAPTER FIFTEEN

KARMI

The heat in my soul on 212 degrees Each lyric hits every
nerve
Blow by blow, one rhyme is laced with just enough
medication to knock me out
No one short of a stranger, yet his words know me personally
When will I have had enough? His lips are smooth like butter
How have these harsh words not bruised them? His face
brightens knowingly-
That what he speaks is me
I inhale with no release, the wrong breath will release the
secret between us
I am amazed at how my beautiful lies smell like
death when told from this stranger's lips I realize that I hate
him,
Him – with his prying mind and knowing eyes
This stranger with familiar words will be no friend of mine

Downtown Houston was unusually still the evening that
Karmi stepped into Red Cat Jazz Café. Although her class
with Donnica was over, she had been in contact with her
via email. Donnica sent her newsletters and updates on

literary events in the area. None of them interested Karmi until she heard about the open mic night.

Karmi's eye caught the illumination of the red cat hanging above the small burgundy canopy that hovered over the entrance. Soft jazz music met her at the register to her right, where she paid the ten-dollar cover charge.

She turned her left ankle to get a better grip on the dark maroon heel she wore to match her blouse and black satin shorts. Her hair was pushed back from her face with a simple black headband.

As Karmi gripped the clutch in her hand, she slid through the small, square tables with black tablecloths draped over them until she came to an empty one in the middle near the wall. At that moment on the stage there were only three musicians: a saxophonist, a bass player, and a drummer. It wasn't her first time in this particular café, but for some reason, everything seemed different.

Right below the stage, passing as the front row, was a white couch with a slight oval curve and plush cushions. It reached each end of the stage. Directly behind the white couch was an identical one, only the cushions were a deep red while the back of the couch was black. A few feet behind them sat the square, two-person tables. Karmi loved the chairs because they were low, comfortable, and draped in black like the tables.

To the right of the stage and tables was a small step up towards a large bar with small, red, illuminating lights hanging above it. There were also more tables between the ceiling-to-floor wooden beams. The walls were red and held several pieces of framed art. There was also a wrap- around couch that went around the wall of that particular section of the café.

To Karmi's left was a large rectangular-shaped hole in the

wall that was completely white; walls, couch, and tables were marked for very important people.

Waitresses passed by each table, taking care of the house's two-item minimum with ease. Karmi was there no longer than twenty minutes before the open mic night started.

A short, thick woman that Karmi knew to be the owner's wife stepped on stage. A few people clapped for her while others nursed their drinks. Her black, natural hair was wrapped up into two tight braids, and she wore a long maxi dress that swept the ground of the stage.

"We want to welcome you all to Red Cat," she said, flashing a smile. "We're going to start tonight's mic session with someone who has been in high demand for the last few months. Devin, please come grace us with your presence."

The woman stepped off the stage as the man of the hour took her place. He wasn't very tall. Even on stage Karmi could tell he was probably her height or just an inch or two taller. He was a light chocolate color that glowed in the fluorescent lights set around the stage. His dark hair was in a low cut with small ringlets of curls peaking from his head. Karmi couldn't see his eyes from where she sat, but his smile was bright. She even smiled at the sight of the small gap between his two front teeth. It gave him a boyish charm but made her want to laugh. He was a little stocky, but his clothes hung on him well. Karmi could see women at tables around her were clearly aroused. She wondered what all the fuss was about.

"I can't believe y'all like me that much," he said.

The crowd laughed. Some even yelled out that they loved him. He bowed his head humbly for a second before clearing his throat and adjusting the microphone stand to the perfect height. He held his left hand out parallel to his waist and held up his index finger. The trio of musicians began to play moderato. Devin ran a hand down his face before exhaling and closing his eyes, stepping closer to the microphone before raising both hands to grip it.

"Hey, young girl, with lips so fine and hips so right, delighting in the slightest movements you provide a fantasy. There's an illusion that you are, what dreams are made of. Hey, young girl, you walk as if the sun shines between your thighs, yet the smile of your face can't be that bright. When you hide behind the Maybelline wondering if your mask is thick enough and on just right."

Karmi shifted in her chair, crossing her legs under the table and turning slightly to the right. While scratching the back of her head, she looked around to gauge everyone's reaction.

"You young girls sway feeble-minded men and curious women to your knees, using those temptations to fill voids that are only left emptier."

His sway as he spoke was filled with authority, and Karmi tried hard not to believe this man had known her all her life and was calling her on her wrongs.

"Hey, young girl. Hey, empty girl with no heart to suffice with emotions you thrive off of, those emotions that men don't steal from you but the ones you let go of willingly. What's wrong with you young girls who thought sharing was caring? Be selfish and learn to keep those for yourself."

The beat of the trio stopped as soon as Devin's hands fell from the microphone. The café erupted in finger snaps, whistles, and howls. Karmi sat motionless as anxiety fell like rain over her body. While Devin announced he would be speaking at a church that following Saturday if anyone wanted to hear more from him, someone came around passing out a flyer for the event.

Karmi cleared her throat, sipped her water, and looked down at the picture of the man who just crushed her soul. He hadn't done anything in particular to her personally; yet, Karmi was ready to go to battle. Her cheeks felt hot, remembering his words and ultimately remembering that she was that young girl. No, she remembered that she *is* that young girl, because although it had been almost a month since she'd had sex with Khalil and was attacked by his wife, nothing in her life was stopping her from a relapse. And that terrified her.

Karmi felt chastised by this man who she didn't even know and wanted to run as far away from him as possible.

But, somehow, she found herself staring at him once again that following Saturday.

Karmi couldn't remember the last time she had been inside of a church. Her mother's spirituality lied within her own home, so Karmi was never forced to spend long hours listening to sermons like people she knew in school.

The church was small and unconventional. It was located in a shopping duplex off of Highway 59 and looked more like the community center than a church. Behind the double doors was a small reception area with a few artificial potted plants, a desk, and a stand with different pamphlets on services offered there. There was a nursery and a few classrooms to the right, and the sanctuary was through the doors on the left.

The sanctuary itself was a large open space with several rows of chairs with dark green cushioning. There was a long, rectangular stage that came up a few inches from the ground; it held two big chairs, another small platform, a podium, and a drum set on the far right end. Quotes and scriptures decorated the wall, but most of it was plain.

Karmi moved through the rows and sat closer to the wall, behind a group of people that were sitting and discussing Devin.

She tried to pry a little to get some information on him but didn't want to join any conversations with strangers.

From what she did hear, Karmi could conclude that he wasn't a pastor or anything like that. So, she wondered how he was allowed to speak in the church so freely.

Once he came in, all conversation stopped.

Karmi didn't even know what she was doing there or what this service consisted of. For some odd reason, the atmosphere reminded her of her mother.

Karmi could remember being younger, before she was eleven. She remembered Neiva knitting quilts with her own mother and how they would talk in their native tongue.

Karmi never learned the language as she should have but knew enough to pick up bits and pieces of their conversations. Karmi believed that was what they wanted anyway.

She remembered being wrapped up in unfinished quilts that already consumed her entire body; you would think they were complete. Neiva would be busy working on one end, reminding Karmi to be very still as to not mess her up. Karmi loved being wrapped up in that blanket. She missed the stillness of it all.

"Thanks for coming," Devin said.

Karmi looked up to see him leaning forward a row in front of her with his hand stretched out. She looked down at it but did not move to respond. He pulled his hand back, awkwardly running it down the denim of his jeans before standing straight up.

"You were at the jazz café, right?" he asked.

Karmi narrowed her eyes and nodded. She looked around to see people leaving. Was it over?

"Well, I'm glad you decided to come. I hope my words changed you."

"Excuse me?" she asked, blinking a few times before her

back hit the metal of the chair as she sat straight up. "Changed me? You don't know me."

The right corner of Devin's mouth turned up into a grin as he looked around to see if anyone else had caught Karmi's outburst.

"Miss, I wasn't implying that I did. Poetry changes in general."

Karmi's face felt hot with embarrassment, but she wouldn't let on that she was wrong.

"Maybe your poetry isn't that good to change someone," she snapped.

Devin's grin dropped before he reached up to rub his ear with his left hand. His lips pursed a little before relaxing, and he then stretched his neck by tilting his head side to side.

"If you believed that you wouldn't be here," he said. "Goodnight."

Karmi opened her mouth for a rebuttal, but Devin smoothly and quickly walked away to acknowledge someone else. Karmi huffed before clutching onto her small bag and jetting out of her seat.

"Who in the hell does he think he is?" she asked herself, her heels pounding hard onto the concrete as she stalked over to her car.

Karmi pulled the handle with force, the door swinging open quickly, and she hoped into the driver's seat.

For some unknown reason, Devin had gotten under Karmi's skin. She was irritated, and it came out in her driving. Houston traffic was not kind to anyone with road rage, but Karmi tried her luck, taking the highway to get home quicker.

Karmi pushed through the front door of her apartment and threw her purse down near the small end table by the door. She turned around in a full circle before securing the locks on the door and kicking her shoes off on top of her purse.

She tapped her hands against the door as that familiar ache in the pit of her stomach began to growl and let her know the desire was building to pacify the humiliation. She shook her head and mouthed the word *no* as she walked away from the door and further into her apartment. The stillness agitated her, so she pressed power on the television for some background noise. Karmi paced the length of her love seat and inhaled before closing her eyes.

"He doesn't know you," she mumbled.

"But everyone knows what you do," she thought. *"Everyone knows what you've done."*

Karmi felt tears fall before she scrambled to the door. She slid down to her knees when the hum in her stomach got louder and then searched for her phone through the miscellaneous items in her way. Once she found it, she grinned while scrolling through her contacts, looking for any name that could be useful to her at the moment.

She stopped at each name, trying to quickly recall where she'd met them and if they would be able to eliminate the hum in the way she would need them to. Before she could pick one, her phone rang.

It was Donnica.

"He-hello?"

"Karmi? Are you busy?"

"No. Actually, I just got home."

"Great!" Donnica said, not hearing the pain in Karmi's voice. "We need to meet soon about a small publishing opportunity."

"Publishing?"

The hum in her stomach was immediately drowned by anxiety.

"Donnica, I don't know."

"Karmi, just come to the meeting," Donnica pleaded. "It's nothing big. It's local, but it's a start. I promise it will be worth it."

Karmi listened to Donnica give a list of reasons why she should be excited. It wasn't much, but monetary compensation would be given. It was Donnica's first business venture as a co-publisher. If nothing else, Donnica thought it would be something fun to do.

The only thing fun in Karmi's life was indulging in sexual pleasures, and as of lately, that seemed to be a false hope. She could use something that classified as *clean* fun.

Karmi sighed before sitting down on the floor with her back against her front door and looking up at the ceiling.

"When is the meeting?"

CHAPTER SIXTEEN

DONNICA

She sighed as Jeremiah pulled her around to stand in front of him by the stove. He wrapped his right hand around her waist as he stirred the mixed vegetables in the saucepan. Placing her head back on his shoulder, she closed her eyes and swayed in his embrace. It felt good for Donnica to be back there.

Last month, Jeremiah moved back into his and Donnica's home, and the legal separation ended.

Jeremiah's practice was steady, so he urged Donnica to take her time with her next book.

She hadn't even thought about writing in a while. Things with Amber and the independent publishing company were going well. She decided to take a break and focus on publishing instead. She even thought about going back to school to finish her degree in English.

Thinking about school led Donnica to think about her family back in Missouri. Undoubtedly, her parents and extended family were disappointed when they found out she had dropped out with only three semesters left to her first degree. Her sister couldn't wait to rub it in her face. When the success of her first best seller hit, however, all that changed.

Everyone called to congratulate her, asked when she was

coming home, and couldn't express enough about how proud they were. In the wake of recent events, the only phone calls Donnica got from her family were ones assuring her that it was all because she hadn't finished school in the first place.

Donnica groaned before smacking her forehead with her open right hand. Jeremiah frowned and asked her what was wrong.

"I forgot Mariah is coming in tomorrow night."

"I haven't seen her since the family reunion," Jeremiah said.

Donnica nodded because she hadn't either. That was two and a half years ago.

Although Mariah was a few years younger, she always thought she was better than Donnica. She'd finished school early and was now working on her second degree. Mariah was twenty-four, and since her life was so figured out, she took pleasure in Donnica's life issues.

"Is she staying here?" Jeremiah asked.

"Just for a couple of days," Donnica said. "I think Mom sent her down here to stick her nose in my business."

Jeremiah laughed before kissing Donnica on her cheek and turning to finish his meal.

Since she'd left Missouri, Donnica's relationship with her immediate family was strained. She'd never been that close to Mariah in anything other than distance. So, when she moved to Texas, Donnica wasn't too upset that she didn't see her every day.

She picked at everything Donnica did; even her accomplishments could have been better. Whenever Donnica tried to point out her sister's behavior to their parents, Mariah always batted her eyelashes and acted as if her intentions were always genuine. Donnica called Mariah innocently annoying.

"I guess I'll spend the weekend in my office," Jeremiah said.

Donnica frowned at his grinning face and slapped his arm. He laughed before hugging her.

"Don't act like that. You know I don't get down with the cat fights, baby."

"I can handle, Mariah."

"Um hum."

The next evening when Donnica was driving circles around Houston Hobby to avoid parking, Mariah called to announce her plane just landed. Not wanting to waste any more gas, Donnica had no choice but to pay the parking fee in the arrival lot and wait for her baby sister. Strike number one.

Determined not to get out and actually venture into the hectic airport, Donnica pulled out her phone and sent Mariah a message with her location. Within ten minutes, Mariah was prancing to the car with a designer duffle bag over her left shoulder and a matching purse dangling from her right hand.

Donnica surveyed her sister as best she could through the tint. The relativity showed through their physical appearance. She had lightened her brown hair with honey blonde highlights and cut a few inches off, which resulted in a layered swing bob that came just below her ears.

Mariah's face was slimmer than Donnica's, and her matching skin tone was free of the freckles that Donnica tried to hide daily. Mariah also got their father's chestnut eyes as Donnica did.

Donnica unlocked her doors just as Mariah pulled the back door open and pushed her bags in. After jumping in the passenger seat, Mariah smiled before reaching over to pat Donnica's exposed thigh. Donnica hissed a little while pulling her shorts down.

"Hey, sissy," Mariah said, buckling her seatbelt. Donnica smiled and tried not to cringe at the nickname.

What Mariah considered a term of endearment always made Donnica feel as if she was questioning her strength.

"How was your flight?" Donnica asked, looking at her peripheral for clearance.

"Not too long. You know I don't do nothing but fall asleep as soon as the plane takes off," Mariah replied, reaching to change the song Donnica was playing.

"I don't see how you sleep through plane rides."

"That's because you worry too much," Mariah said. "Feed me!"

Laughing, Donnica shook her head before pulling out onto the highway.

When Donnica and Mariah were younger, before they even made it to grade school, their mother taught them a game she used to play with her sister. They called it

Thumbs. No one else could ever make sense of it. They'd place their fists side by side with their thumbs pressed

together at the pad. They'd push down on each other's thumb and the first one whose hand shook the hold lost. Whoever won was allowed to say or do anything they wanted without the loser snitching or fighting back.

As soon as Donnica pulled into her driveway, Mariah turned sideways towards her and held her fist out. Donnica tilted her head to the left and sighed heavily.

"Really, Mariah?"

"Yes, really, Donnica. I haven't seen you in two years. Come on!" she said, lifting her fist in the air higher to emphasis her point.

Donnica rolled her eyes before pushing her thumb into Mariah's.

"You are such a cheater," Mariah said, pushing back. Donnica smirked before looking back at their fists.

Mariah's nose flared a little before Donnica lost her focus and her fist shifted to the right. She mumbled a curse as the siblings got out of the car and she helped Mariah with her bags.

"What do you want?" Donnica asked, after they quickly retreated out of the Houston evening heat and into the house.

Mariah looked around with a smug expression on her face and then walked further into the foyer, dropping her bag along the wall before it hit the floor.

"Where's Jeremiah?"

"At his office. He's working late."

"But he *does* live here," Mariah said, turning to face her older sister with a smirk. "Right?"

Donnica's eyes shifted as she keyed in the alarm code and glanced at her sister. She hadn't told anyone in her family about the separation besides her mother in general conversation. Had she revealed that private information with Mariah, even though she'd promised not to?

"Mariah, don't be stupid. Of course, he lives here. He's my husband."

Donnica walked briskly past Mariah and into the kitchen. She wondered why she felt like she was lying when her statement had been one hundred percent true. She looked into a drawer filled with menus and pulled one out for a local pizzeria.

Mariah leaned against the doorframe while Donnica ordered a large sausage pizza, one half with pepperoni and the other with pineapple. She added an order of hot wings just in case Jeremiah hadn't eaten lunch and wanted a big dinner.

"So Ma told me about the class you had to teach for going

Jazmine Sullivan on your boss' car," Mariah said. "How's that going?"

Donnica shook her head to ignore the song reference and her incident with Steve Point's Audi.

"It's over actually, but it was a very mind-opening opportunity. I've gotten some good network contacts from it for my next project."

Donnica didn't really want to tell Mariah about the publishing company, but she also wanted some type of satisfaction in everyone knowing that the class hadn't been a total waste of time.

Mariah tapped her long acrylic fingernails against the granite counter top and sighed. She looked at Donnica with narrowed eyes and tilted her head just a little. Donnica stared blankly back at her for several minutes before Mariah huffed.

"Geez, D! Give it up already! When did you and Jeremiah get back together?"

"I don't know what Mom told you…" Donnica started but was cut off.

"What you should have told me!" Mariah said, twisting her neck as she spoke.

Donnica chewed on her bottom lip before rolling her eyes.

"What happened between Jeremiah and me should not be a topic you all discuss at lunch."

"Why are you being so formal with me?" Mariah asked, holding her head back and placing her hand over her chest. "Like we aren't sisters."

"I'm not married to you. This ain't your business."

Donnica knew it was time to end the discussion when she began to use words that an editor would kill her over. Like a ringing bell in a high school hallway, the alarm beeped that the front door was ajar, and Jeremiah's deep tone flowed through the foyer.

"I'm home!"

Donnica smiled for two reasons: that Jeremiah was actually home and the fact that he'd announced it. Mariah eyed her sister before smiling and turning to go greet her brother-in-law. Donnica stayed in the kitchen.

"There's my favorite brother-in-law!" Mariah said.

Donnica rolled her eyes at her sister's sarcasm because they did not have any other siblings. "It's going to be a long weekend."

Donnica's BlackBerry beeped twice, and she hurried to pull it from her purse, thankful for the distraction. She smiled to see Amber was calling.

"Have you checked your email tonight?" Amber asked, the urgency in her voice making Donnica frown.

"I just got in from picking my sister up from the airport," Donnica said. "What's up?"

"Well, I know you talked to your girl about the meeting for the poetry collection. She emailed us a few pieces to look over. Donnica, you were right about her."

Amber went on about Karmi's poetry, and Donnica couldn't help but smile with pride. She was well aware that Karmi had a raw ability to make her readers fall in love with her poetry and feel all of her emotions.

Karmi's work reminded Donnica of a modern day Sylvia Plath. Donnica always felt empathy for Plath's work. It was very dark at times, but it was something so real about the emotion in it that even if Donnica hadn't gone through any situation similar to the poem, she could feel exactly how it felt.

Karmi laid her emotions in her poetry, and it was something so beautiful disturbed that Donnica wished she knew more about the young woman's life. However, she wouldn't dare impose by asking.

"I'll check them out in the morning. How many were there?"

"Just four, but she said she'd bring more to the meeting. So she's serious?"

"Seems to be." Donnica sighed, sitting down on the stool and leaning over the counter with her elbows. As she cradled the phone between her shoulder and ear, she caught a glimpse of Jeremiah walking through the threshold of the kitchen. She bit her bottom lip while Jeremiah licked his.

Amber went on talking and even Mariah was rambling aimlessly, but it seemed as if Jeremiah's presence blocked out everything else at the moment.

It was how it had been since they reunited, and Donnica was excited about it.

"Yes, it sounds like we're making progress, but I'll call you in the morning after I read them," Donnica said, standing up as Jeremiah rounded the counter to approach her.

After she hung up with Amber, she sat the phone down and wrapped her arms around his neck. Jeremiah gripped her hips and kissed her. Donnica smiled against his lips before sitting back down on the stool and moving her arms from his neck to around his waist.

"Thought you were going to stay locked up in your office all night," Donnica said.

"Felt like seeing you sooner," he responded with a shrug.

Donnica sighed before laying her head on his chest. She turned to see Mariah looking at them.

"You hungry, big head?"

"Yes! How long does it take a pizza to cook?" she asked, stomping her foot before walking off towards the living room.

"You order me some hot wings, babe?" Jeremiah asked, looking down at his wife.

She smiled and nodded.

Whenever you make efforts to learn and grow from your past, it always resurfaces to show you that you haven't gone far enough. It does not let us forget what we are emerging from. While rewriting and editing the chapters of your life, make sure you keep your eye on the current page. We begin to break down our behavior and the reasons we were there in the first place. While we grow, sometimes we never expect to see others around us doing the same.

CHAPTER SEVENTEEN

LANGSTON

When Langston walked up to Renee's front door, he could hear music blasting through the walls. He stepped onto the green mat, leaning closer to the door before the song became recognizable as the theme song for one of Kayla's favorite shows.

Two other distinct voices singing in different keys were Kayla and Renee. Langston shook his head and chuckled before he rang the doorbell. Renee stopped singing, but Kayla continued. Thumps across Renee's hardwood floor let Langston know where she was before she opened the door. She smiled and pushed her hair back with her left hand. She then let her hand fall to her chest before it dropped to her side.

"Hey," she said, quickly pushing air from her mouth a few times. Renee stepped aside and Langston walked in the house. "Mini-Me, look who's here!"

"Daddy, my show isn't over yet," Kayla said, never taking her eyes off of the television screen.

Renee threw both of her hands up in a mock surrender when Langston gave her an eye. He took the moment to observe her attire. Renee was wearing dark brown leggings that stopped above her ankles and a bright yellow t-shirt that had a smiling face drawn on it. Langston recognized the outfit as something Renee regularly wore to lounge around the house.

"She made me record it. She even went into the menu and played it herself," Renee said, shutting and locking the door once Langston was fully into the living room.

"I heard you in here singing with her," he said, taking a seat in the recliner near the wall.

Renee's light maple cheeks reddened before she turned to hide her embarrassment.

Langston smiled at her. "Go on and finish."

"No, she got it," Renee said, walking off towards the hallway.

Langston got up and followed behind her. Renee turned and disappeared into Kayla's bedroom. As Langston followed, he noticed a few framed pictures on the wall.

Most of them were of Kayla alone doing random things, but a few were of the two together.

Langston stopped in front of one and ran his finger over it. They were sitting on a chair, and Kayla was on Renee's lap. Kayla's left hand was pinching Renee's nose while Renee's eyes were wide open, allowing full view of her thick, curled eyelashes, and her cheeks were puffed out. Kayla had her tongue sticking out towards Renee and her other hand reaching towards the ceiling.

When Langston laughed, Renee stuck her head out of Kayla's bedroom and frowned.

"What?"

"Who took this?" he asked, pointing to the picture with his index finger and looking at Renee.

She looked at the picture and smiled.

"My mom did. I just printed all these a few days ago," she said, then ducked back into Kayla's room.

Langston went in to see her packing Kayla's backpack.

"Felt like the walls were empty, you know?"

"That's what's up," he said, handing her a pair of jeans that were folded on the bed.

"I want a picture of all of us together," Renee said, still looking down into the bag. "Nothing big, just something she can have, you know?"

Langston looked at her, wondering if she still thought she was trying to put her family back together as she had admitted to doing at the courthouse. The last time the three had taken pictures together was when Kayla was six months old. Langston remembered because one of the photos was still visible as soon as he opened his wallet. That was when they were actually a family, though. Now that was definitely not what they were. However, he was Kayla's dad and Renee was her mother.

"That doesn't sound too bad," he said.

Renee nodded before zipping up Kayla's bag. "How you been, though? Everything cool?"

Renee sighed before wiping her hands down her thighs and nodding. "It's been an adjustment, but I'll admit that I love having her here," she said.

Langston's heart suffered a small fracture at remembering that he felt the exact same way when asked about their previous living arrangements. He was still not okay with Kayla not staying with him, and although it was childish of him, he often wished Kayla gave Renee a harder time than she had.

It was as if in a matter of weeks, Kayla went from a pure daddy's girl to being attached to Renee. Langston knew it was all about the time spent, but he still desired a little loyalty. He felt silly because he still saw her almost every weekend and she still loved him.

Sometimes it just wasn't the same.

But, Langston knew what Renee's plan was, and at the moment, it didn't sound like a bad deal. If they could work it out, if Langston could get past how Renee pretty much disowned him and their daughter until this newfound motherhood crept into her system, then they could be a family.

Kayla would have them both all day everyday, and he wouldn't have to be the one suffering while away from his little girl.

"Daddy, come sing with me!" Kayla shouted from the living room.

"Mommy wants to," Langston said.

Renee frowned and gave him an eye while Kayla called for her instead. Langston laughed as Renee's feet dragged against the carpet as she left her bedroom.

Langston picked up the backpack and carried it with him into the living room. He sat it down on the other side of the couch and then watched Renee unenthusiastically mock Kayla's dance moves. Their arms flailed out from their sides as they hopped side to side.

"Why does it seem like these songs never end?" Renee asked, looking back at Langston.

"Because they're awesome!" Kayla said.

Langston reminded her that she was inside and to stop yelling. Her voice retracted a little, but she kept jumping around.

Renee finally gave up and sat down next to Langston. "She's way too hyper, and I didn't even give her sugar cereal today," Renee said.

Langston laughed but shook his head, already seeing how the rest of his day was going to go with an overactive four-year-old.

"Hey, I need a favor."

"What?"

"Tomorrow is friends and family day at my church."

"But I'm supposed to have Kayla all weekend," Langston said, cutting her off.

Her nose flared a little before she rolled her eyes. "You didn't let me finish. I was going to say I want both of you to come."

"Me?" Langston asked. "Renee, you know I don't do church."

"Please? It's just a couple of hours, and there's a dinner afterwards. So, you won't even have to worry about what to eat tomorrow," Renee said, biting her lip. "I really want you guys there."

As Langston's eyes roamed her face, his resistance softened. She still had it, but everything inside him wanted to fight it.

"Fine," he said. Renee squealed a little and clapped her hands.

In that moment, Langston remembered a poem of Karmi's that he read while in the creative writing class. She rarely shared her poetry then, and at the time, he hadn't known how powerful her words were. He almost felt ashamed of how much she had touched him with the style she wrote in. It was usually only women who got so attached to poetry.

Knowing her as a friend now and realizing there was more to her story, it made her words worth more. He recalled the poem starting off as a cliché—a girl running through a field of flowers, pushing the tips of her fingers along the petals as she made her way towards the end of it. Only the light dimmed and the flowers began to die as she touched them. Everything around her darkened and she couldn't see her way. Only she came upon a light that was so bright but seemed so far away. She pushed her way through the darkness and made it to the light. The light was so energetic and warming that she forgot the darkness she had to go through to get there.

As Langston watched Renee and Kayla, he knew he had to stop second-guessing Renee's transformation. It had been a couple of months since the custody hearing, and Renee hadn't proved otherwise. Langston knew she had started going to church, and although he questioned it before, he realized he had no authority to. How could he question someone else trying to change their life when he was doing the same thing?

Langston had no idea if he was even interested in starting something with Renee again. The benefits presented themselves in a comfortable situation for his daughter, but was he willing to go through the pain of her leaving again when she felt life as they knew it was too much?

"I'm ready!"

Langston smiled as Kayla plopped down on his lap, panting a little from her singing workout.

"I'm going to head to the laundromat since you guys are heading out," Renee said.

Langston nodded as he bent down to grab Kayla's bag, and Renee kissed her on top of her head.

"See you later, Kay." "Later, Mommy."

Renee and Langston laughed a little at Kayla's vernacular before he and Kayla headed out the front door.

No matter how hard we press delete in our lives, sometimes the mental stain never fades. We clean up our new pages, making them look decent and presentable, but inside, we still feel as if those old pages are being ridiculed and criticized. Often when others accept the new us, we don't allow ourselves to accept the new them. We are hesitant because we don't want to end up writing the same story with different words.

CHAPTER EIGHTEEN

KARMI

*I keep her outside of the tarnished safe of my truth The only
righteous piece of my world left untouched
With no effort of mine, she makes my soul alright Never
having to dream of life without her
She is loving, protective, irreplaceable Annoying,
inappropriate, stubborn
Yet, I am sure everything that is good in the world has been
filtered now into her being
Just for me to witness
The indefinite warmth of an unconditional love I cannot cope
without her*

"So what are you going to do today, Karmiti?"

Karmi looked up at Dr. Reynolds, making sure to give her eye contact. She had cancelled her last two appointments in an attempt to self-medicate, but in light of recent events, Karmi felt it was time to see her again.

Karmi could not shake the shame she felt when Devin approached her at his church. It had started out as annoyance and irritation, but as the days passed, Karmi felt as if her soul was dying. How easily it was for a complete stranger to decipher her lifestyle in a matter of minutes.

She wasn't used to caring about what people thought, and

she had come up with only one possible conclusion as to why Devin's words were bugging her so badly.

She wasn't happy with herself.

She wasn't satisfied with how her life was going, and it was all because of how her life had gone. She had to handle the feelings from her past, and there was only one way to do so.

"Today, I'm going to tell my mother," she said, mumbling her words at first before sitting up straight and repeating herself.

"What are you going to tell your mother?" Dr. Reynolds asked.

Karmi's chin dipped a little as she blinked a few times before swallowing the saliva gathering in her mouth.

"I'm going to tell my mother that when I was twelve years old, my dad's college buddy began to touch me inappropriately," Karmi said, looking at her therapist for confirmation.

Dr. Reynolds only nodded.

"We hadn't seen him much until after my father's funeral. He was always calling to ask my mom if she needed anything and that he would always be there. He began to come around so much that my mom often left me with him when she had to work. She trusted him because Dad did."

"How did that make you feel?" Dr. Reynolds asked. "Like I was supposed to trust him," Karmi answered. "Like I was supposed to make sure Neiva's trust didn't change."

Karmi frowned and shook her head at how many times she'd taken up for Hassun, thinking it was the right thing to do. Dr. Reynolds urged her to go on. She exhaled before nodding.

"He didn't stop touching me but forced me to reciprocate. I'm going to tell her that I was molested for nearly three years before Hassun's job transferred him out of town, and I never said anything about it because I didn't want her to look at him any different than my dad did."

She finally began to cry. Even though she felt she'd cried enough, the tears would not end. Karmi violently wiped her face, but it was drenched again in seconds. Her mouth felt sticky, and her nose began to run. She shook her head, but Dr. Reynolds protested.

"Just let your feelings run their course, Karmiti. You only did what you thought was right."

"But it was wrong!" Karmi yelled. "My intentions don't matter if it's wrong in the end."

"Why do you feel that way?"

"I wouldn't feel *this* way if it was right."

Dr. Reynolds only nodded and Karmi sighed. She hated that Dr. Reynolds never gave an actual opinion, even if she knew it was only her job to guide Karmi's feelings and help her make her own decisions.

Dr. Reynolds looked at Karmi over the rim of her glasses and poked her bottom lip out a little before sucking it back in. She waited a few moments until Karmi's cries were controlled and then gave her an assuring smile.

"Let's talk about your mother. How do you think she's going to take the news?"

"I'm so scared to tell her," Karmi admitted. "She confided in him so much after my father died. She treated him like family."

"How do you think this will affect your relationship?"

Karmi bit her lip and shook her head softly. She had kept it in for years. Hassun left when she was fifteen, and with her twenty-second birthday nearing, it was time to stop worrying about her mother's feelings concerning it all.

"I don't know," Karmi said. "But, I have to get this off of me."

"Coming clean about something you've held in for years is never easy. You've gone over and over in your head about how the interaction will go and how it could possibly solve all that is wrong in your life, but the reality is you don't know how she's going to react," Dr. Reynolds said, as Karmi took in her words. "You've accepted the past and plan to move on from it, but not everyone is on the same page as you when it comes to growth."

"So what do I do if she doesn't accept it?" Karmi asked, her mixed feelings allowing frustration to fill her mind.

"This is going to be extremely difficult," Dr. Reynolds advised. "However, I believe it's a great step in the right direction. Now, we don't meet until next week, but you call me if you need me after this."

Karmi nodded, taking the advice and the time as the end of their session. She inhaled before grabbing her purse from the back of the leather chair and walked slowly out of the office. Karmi mentally mapped out the directions from the office to her mom's home, knowing if she did not do this now she would not do it at all.

She'd have to take Fort Bend to get there quickly. So, she shuffled through the armrest to get enough change to pass through the toll station. Although she stayed in downtown Houston, Karmi was glad her mom still stayed in Missouri City. It wasn't as fast paced as where she stayed, so she knew when she needed a break from the world, her mother's place was where she could go.

Hopefully that didn't change.

She felt childish, but the moment Karmi pulled up in front of her mom's house, she wished she had her blanket with her. It was near ninety degrees outside, but if she could wear it as a coat she would, just to feel secure. The front door was open and Karmi could see through the screen door. She hated when Neiva left the door open as if she were trying to supply her neighborhood with the cool air from her central air unit. Karmi shook her head as she locked her car door and closed it. It was almost as if her mind was trying to focus on everything except what she had to tell her mother.

When Karmi entered the house, Neiva was walking past the foyer and into the kitchen. She stopped at the sound of her door being opened and gave Karmi a knowing smile.

"I figured you would be over here after your appointment," Neiva said, continuing into the kitchen.

Karmi gave her a weak smile in return. Instead of going into the kitchen to see what Neiva was cooking, she opted to take a seat on the couch in the living room.

The old wool couch had been turned more catty corner to the fireplace that was never used anymore. The matching loveseat sat further away, and the wooden coffee table was still in front of the couch. It was a dark oak color with occasional darker brown lines going through its interior, giving off the impression that it was carved directly from a tree with no extra treatments. It always looked as if you could get a splinter from it, but whenever Karmi ran her hand over it, the surface was always smooth.

Neiva never kept a television in the living room, and Karmi was sure she rarely watched the one in her room. The house that usually held a peaceful quiet for Karmi was suffocating her all of a sudden.

"Mommy," Karmi called from her spot on the couch, "I need to talk to you about something."

The few seconds it took Neiva to walk from the kitchen into the living room went by agonizingly slow for Karmi. Neiva stood in the doorway with a rag in hand, wiping her hands. She had on a long brown dress with the sleeves cut off. Her long grey hair was pulled back into an underhanded French braid, almost as it always was. She gave Karmi a warm smile before nodding.

"I need you to sit down, though," Karmi said.

The smile faded from Neiva's face as she took a seat on the other end of the couch.

"What's wrong, Karmiti?"

"I have to tell you something."

"Baby, you already said that," Neiva said.

Nodding, Karmi knew she was stalling for time, but there was no more time.

"Mommy, after Dad's funeral something horrible happened to me."

She paused to gauge her mother's reaction to her words so far, but only a look of confusion graced Neiva's face. She was hoping this would be easier to say, but she hadn't known why she thought that way. This was the hardest thing she ever had to do.

"I was molested," Karmi told her. "A lot." Then she thought, *Who says that?*

Karmi mentally kicked herself. She had rehearsed this in her mind several times. It hadn't even been a whole hour since she'd left Dr. Reynolds' office and said exactly what she wanted to say.

"Karmiti, you shouldn't say things like that," Neiva said. "That was a hard time for all of us."

"It was an even harder time for me," Karmi mumbled, looking down at the chipped fingernail polish on her nails.

She was usually anal about the upkeep of her manicure. She picked at the painting on her left thumb with the nail of her index finger and watched a few chips fall onto the fabric of her jeans.

"Child, this is ridiculous. The only man around us at that time was Hassun."

And with recognition in her eyes, Neiva had figured it out. His name from someone else's lips didn't sound as menacing at it had in Karmi's head. She was glad she didn't have to say it.

"You can't be serious."

Karmi's heart dropped as a blur of words fell from her lips. She told Neiva about the three years of confusion and lies that Hassan had produced. How many times she wanted to tell her, but Hassan would always bring up some great memory of her dad and make Neiva smile all day from thoughts of her beloved husband.

She couldn't do it to her mother then, not when she was the only one left in her life that truly loved her.

However, Karmi was tired of battling within herself on the same issue for years.

"I don't believe you."

Karmi had prepared herself to hear her mother say that, but it didn't hurt any less. She stood up from the couch as if she had been stuck with a needle filled with the type of chemicals used on prisoners on death row. Her stomach twisted, but she swallowed hard to repress the urge to vomit.

"This has been eating away at my soul for years," Karmi said. "I would not lie about it."

"If it were true, Karmiti, why would you just now tell me?" Neiva asked, placing her right hand over her heart and looking around her living room with shifty eyes. "Why would you allow him to be around us in that way?"

"I was twelve."

"You knew right from wrong!"

Karmi stumbled back as if she'd been pushed. Her heart banged against her chest, and she felt it move up into her throat. Her face and neck felt hot first before it began to pulse through her body. If her mother were implying what Karmi thought she was, this would not end well.

"I was…I was trying to protect you," Karmi said, now knowing this was not a good idea at all.

All emotion drained from Neiva's face. It was clear she held no sympathy for her only child at the moment, and Karmi could feel it from where she stood.

"Are you sure I'm the one you were trying to protect?"

Karmi had had enough. She didn't want to disrespect her mother, so it was time to go home. Her chest heaved up and down as she grabbed her purse. Karmi tried to steady it by patting her chest softly. Reluctantly, she leaned down and kissed Neiva's cheek, but she did not budge. Karmi stood up and sighed.

"I said what I came to say."

CHAPTER NINETEEN

DONNICA

The cotton blend sheets felt cool under Donnica's body as she sat up with her laptop open in front of her.

Jeremiah was still sleeping, so she tried not to make too much noise. The white numbers in the lower right hand corner of her screen told Donnica it was nearing seven in the morning on December 14th. She hadn't known Christmas was coming so soon and was ultimately thankful she only had a few people to shop for.

This was usually a great time to pound out a few hundred words with no direction and hope something great arose from it, but now that Donnica had more pressing issues other than writing, she used this time for business.

Going through her emails, Donnica saved any attachment from Karmi into a special folder on her desktop. Amber hadn't been lying when she said Karmi's poetry was progressing. Donnica could tell it was deeper and held a certain aspect of reality that made it raw and genuine.

She went through a few more poems before making notes of things to talk to Amber about later in the day.

They would be busy most of the morning. Not only was Mariah's plane leaving early afternoon, Amber and Donnica had a meeting with a few possible investors for their company. She had been nervous about the meeting, and her younger sister's visit had not made things any easier.

Deciding she had spent enough time in bed, Donnica got up and prepared herself for the day. Fighting the Houston heat was something Donnica was accustomed to but still didn't like. She opted for a pair of denim shorts and a white, short-sleeve blouse. She hated wearing undershirts, but since the top was a little sheer, she'd have to suffer that day. Once dressed, she grabbed her favorite pair of Coach sandals and headed downstairs towards the sound of the living room television. Mariah was lounging on the couch restlessly.

"About time," Mariah said.

"It's only a little after eight," Donnica mentioned, her finger combing the wrap out of her hair until it laid down right.

She was not up for Mariah's attitude on her last day visiting. Mariah shrugged before sitting up and wiggling her toes.

"What are we doing before I leave?"

Donnica slid her cell phone into her left front pocket and shrugged her shoulders.

"We really only have time to eat before I have to head to the meeting. I can drop you off at a mall before I go."

She almost couldn't help but laugh at the glare Mariah gave her.

"You expect me to walk around a mall by myself for more than an hour?"

"Jeremiah has to work. So, it's either that or you sit here bored," Donnica said, amused at her sister's irritation.

"I can't go to the press conference with you?" Mariah asked.

Donnica gave her a dead stare while chewing on the inside of her bottom lip. It was only an hour and a half, but Donnica just knew Mariah would find some way to make it seem longer. She was already nervous about the media questioning her and Amber anyway. It might not be a good idea to add her current personal stress to that mix, but since Jeremiah could not make it, maybe having Mariah there would provide some type of support.

"Fine," Donnica said with an exhausted sigh.

Mariah's full grin spread as she clapped her hands before standing up.

"Let me go get ready."

Donnica shook her head before walking into her office to collect her things. She smiled a little once she heard the heavy footsteps entering and soon felt her favorite pair of lips on the side of her forehead.

"Mo is running around upstairs talking to herself," Jeremiah said, before laughing. "You're letting her go with you?"

"She pulled my arm," Donnica told him, turning to kiss her husband.

"Yeah, I bet. You be good today."

"I promise," Donnica said, holding her right hand over her heart.

Jeremiah smiled while shaking his head as he walked out of the room.

Donnica and Amber were currently working out of their home offices, so Amber secured a meeting hall at the Doubletree Hilton Hotel downtown for the media conference. When Donnica pulled up, she could already see a few media vans parked along the front of the hotel.

"Are you guys expecting a lot of people?" Mariah asked, as Donnica pulled around the back to the entrance Amber instructed her to go to.

Donnica shook her head. "I know she has this PR guy working to get us press, so I guess so."

"Are you guys even close to publishing anyone?" Mariah asked.

Donnica glanced at her before turning her phone on silent. "Yes."

The minutes before the conference went by in a blur for Donnica. She watched Amber move through the crowd flawlessly, smiling at everyone and shaking hands. She introduced Donnica to people as her partner, and all Donnica could do was smile and nod most of the time.

Mariah had taken a seat in the back to go unnoticed. Once Amber and Donnica made it to their seats on the small stage, Amber covered the microphone in front of her.

"Girl, are you okay?" Amber asked, her dark bangs swaying as she turned towards Donnica.

Donnica's ears rang a little as she tried to keep eye contact with Amber, who patted Donnica's thigh and gave her an assuring smile.

"Just chill, D," Amber said, before sitting straight up again. "Chill."

She gave Donnica a second before she announced that the questioning could begin. One reporter stood up quickly.

"Why did you leave Point Set?" he asked.

Donnica looked at Amber and she nodded. Amber smiled a little before leaning forward.

"I think a lot of big publishers have forgotten the reason we are in this business in the first place," Amber answered. "It's to get the wonderful words of these amazing authors out to the public. It shouldn't be about the money at all. We want to get back to that."

"The media has been buzzing about Donnica's exit from the company. What does that have to do with this merger?"

"We all know I didn't leave on the best of terms," Donnica said, causing a few of them to laugh. "But, it helped me realize that along the way I had gotten sucked into the money machine and away from my true passion. I still want to write, but when Amber presented this opportunity for us to help others realize their dream as I had already, I couldn't pass it up."

"What does Afterlight mean?"

Donnica and Amber traded off answering question after question.

Amber and Donnica had thought long and hard about the name of their company. This was a second chance for them to make some type of historic mark on the literary world that they both loved so much.

They knew it wasn't all about the writing. Going through the process with Point Set taught them that it was only the easy part, especially when a fall from grace presented a challenging position.

"Do you have any authors lined up?"

"We are currently working on a poetry collection that will be our first published piece. We are also soliciting manuscripts for a novel."

"So I guess we can assume that with your latest failed novels, Donnica, you won't be publishing any of your own work?"

Donnica blinked a few times, trying to make sure she'd heard the question right. Amber looked at her with pleading eyes, but Donnica shook her off.

"I've paid my dues to the writing community, and I feel no reason to answer that," Donnica replied.

A few murmurs arose in the audience as Amber's back hit her chair.

"Donnica, don't."

"Are you justifying your latest failures?" another reporter asked.

"I'm simply saying that Afterlight Publishing is not a way for me to redeem my career, as you are trying to portray."

"Any other questions?" Amber asked with a tight lip. Donnica sighed.

"With both of you coming from such a large publishing house, aren't you afraid your company simply will not be big enough?"

"We have a determined team and excellent talent," Amber responded. "Afterlight Publishing will be fine."

Donnica looked around as the crowd dissembled and Amber closed her briefcase. She could tell Amber was upset with how she handled the criticism.

"Amber, I'm sorry."

"When are you going to learn, D?" Amber said, finally turning towards Donnica. She stood on the left end of the small table with her palms pressed into the wood. "You can't say anything you want to say."

"They were out of line," Donnica retorted, keeping her eyes on Mariah, who was making her way to the front of the room where they were.

"It's the media! They will always be out of line," Amber said, frustrated. "You just make sure you stay in line. We'll be fine."

Donnica nodded before she and Amber hugged. Amber said goodbye to Mariah, who was standing across from Donnica on the other side of the table, swinging her arms and letting the fist of her left hand fall into her open right hand.

"Flight leaves soon," Mariah said. Donnica nodded before standing up. "No smart remarks?" Donnica asked.

Mariah smiled. "Nope," she said. "You did enough of that yourself."

Cars filtered out the lanes of I-45 as Donnica tried to navigate through the traffic as quickly as possible. Not only did she want to make sure Mariah got to her flight on time, but she was ready to be alone. Although Mariah hadn't said much since they left the hotel, Donnica knew what she was thinking.

Her temper was horrible, and it made her wonder why she had ventured into the writing business in the first place. Anything dealing with entertainment would be criticized, and Donnica hadn't realized how bad she was at receiving criticism until her failed novels.

Things had been all good when *No Spaces* was released.

Mariah cracked her neck as she reached for her purse when Donnica pulled up into the departure lane.

"You have everything?" Donnica asked.

Mariah nodded before looking at her for a second. "Hey, don't sweat what those reporters were saying," Mariah told her.

Donnica sighed and shook her head. "I'm not. Just leave it alone please."

"I know you better than you think I do," Mariah said, opening the door. "You don't always have to be so defensive."

Donnica nodded before leaning over to hug Mariah. She waited until she pulled her bag from the backseat and walked past the automatic doors of the entrance before pulling away from the curb.

We listen to criticism; we wave it off as misunderstands and we go on with our original plan. Deeper and deeper we pull ourselves into mistakes and issues, and because we know what is supposed to be there, we never see them. No matter how many times someone else points out an error in the book of your life, it will not matter until you recognize it.

CHAPTER TWENTY

LANGSTON

The more Langston thought about his plans for the day, the more the headache increased. He had worked ten days straight and realized that his only off day would be spent taking care of things he could no longer avoid. He hadn't returned any of Alisha's calls, and he hadn't talked to Karmi since his brother confronted him about her.

It was time to get some things straightened out.

Langston invited Alisha out to breakfast that morning at a local restaurant next to the home décor store. When he arrived, she was already in the booth that had backs shaped like old school cars. The restaurant was famous for its fast, good food and old time feel.

Alisha smiled when she saw him and stood up. Langston hugged her and kissed her cheek before she attempted to kiss his lips. He didn't want her to feel awkward, but at the same time, he didn't want to lead her on.

"I feel like I haven't spoken to you in weeks," Alisha said, smiling and obviously exaggerating. Langston laughed a little before he looked down at her plate. "Sorry, I couldn't wait. I have to go to work after this."

"This early?" he asked, knowing she was in the club business along with Jus.

"Yes. I have a meeting for a potential event someone wants me to plan at the club," she said.

Langston nodded, knowing it was something Alisha had been trying to venture off into. He sighed before ordering a cup of coffee once the waitress came to his aid.

"We need to talk."

Alisha's smiled dropped before she sighed. Her blonde highlights became a little more visible as she dipped her chin and rolled her head to the side, looking up at Langston and biting her lip.

"Should have seen this coming," she said. "It's not what you think."

"I think you want to stop seeing me, is what I think. I should have known you were spending way too much time with that girl."

Langston laughed, almost confused at what Alisha was referring to until he realized she was assuming he and Karmi were more than friends.

"First of all, I wasn't lying when I said I was just friends with her. So, don't kid yourself."

"So what's the problem then?" Alisha asked with tight lips. She clapped her hands together and let them fall on the table.

"I've decided to get back with Renee." Alisha blinked a few times and frowned.

"You're kidding me, right? You can't be serious." "I need to be there for my daughter."

"How is that even a possibly good reason to get back with the woman who played you?" Alisha asked, her voice rising in volume.

Langston shook his head as his rounded nose flared a little. He ran his hand down his face before licking his lips.

"You like me, right?" Alisha asked, her eyes pleading and her tone now softer.

Langston nodded.

"Well, what's the problem?"

"I miss my daughter," he admitted.

"That's something you need to sit down and talk to her mother about, L. Not up and get back with her just so you can see your child when you want!"

"You don't understand," he said, growing tired of trying to make her see why he'd made the decision he'd made.

He knew nobody would approve of it, and Alisha was the only one he felt deserved the truth. Everyone else would get the lie he'd concocted that he just wanted to give Renee another chance. It was actually only half a lie, anyway.

"Kayla is not going to be happy if the person she loves most in the world isn't happy. You can't pretend with her. She'll know you aren't happy," Alisha told him.

Langston sat up straight before pulling money from his back pocket. A tear slid down Alisha's face. While wiping it away, she looked out of the window for a second. Cars flew by on the highway next to the restaurant as the sun brightened up the day a little more.

Alisha's words held weight. Langston knew the four- year-old that held his heart knew him better than anyone. However, it was killing him not to see her every day or read to her and listen to her attempts to correct him all the time. It was tearing him up inside not to see how her little face glowed and her eyes lit up when he came to pick her up from school each day. If he had to get back with Renee to make those pains go away, then that was what he had to do.

"I'll make sure she won't."

Alisha nodded slightly before getting up and walking out of the restaurant. Langston stayed behind to pay for her meal. As if he didn't have enough issues to deal with, Jus called in panic mode.

"Man, Jess and Ryan are trying to throw me a party!"

Langston laughed at his brother's dramatic antics and sighed.

"You are graduating soon," Langston said.

"Exactly, which is why I don't want them planning anything for me," Jus said. "You remember Mom's birthday?"

Langston laughed hard while remembering how his mother had gone off on his sister Jessie for how her 65th birthday party was uneventful. Jessie seemed to think she had a knack for party planning and usually dragged her husband into the mess with her. Langston knew there was no way "life-of-the-party" Claude Justin would let his boring sister throw his graduation party.

"You have to talk her out of it," Jus pleaded with his older brother.

Langston nodded, ready to get off the phone and handle the other thing that had been bothering him. "I'll call her later."

Langston waited for the waitress to bring back his change before he hurried out of the restaurant. His breakfast with Alisha was shorter than expected, so he took the extra time to pay a few bills. He stopped at a local grocery store near his home and paid his electric and water bill. Langston usually paid his cell phone bill by phone, but this day, he opted to go to the Sprint store in the mall.

The automatic payment kiosk was his best option since all of the sales associates were unavailable. He laughed a little and shook his head, thinking about how every time he entered the store for a technical problem it would be an all-day event.

Langston wasn't due to meet Karmi at Marble Slab until one o'clock, so he went shopping for his baby girl. For some odd reason, Jus' voice popped in his head about how he wasn't an average father.

While looking through the kids' section in Foot Locker, Langston realized he wasn't. He hadn't known when this adoration for his child became so strong, but it must have been around the time Renee opted out of her parental responsibilities. He knew then that he had to be more for his daughter. Kayla had done nothing wrong.

He resented most of his family that told him he was too young to be raising a child by himself. He thought it quite ironic how society often looked down on men who weren't there for their children. Here he was doing what he knew was right, and he was still getting backlash for it.

Langston ended up buying two pairs of shoes and a few shirts for himself and Kayla before heading out to meet Karmi.

This time, he arrived at his destination before his guest.

Langston picked a small table in the middle near the back and watched Karmi walk in. She was wearing an oversized burgundy t-shirt that had the word "HARVARD" on it in gold letters. He could tell she had cut the collar at the top so it would hang over her left shoulder, revealing the sleeve of a black tank top. Her leggings were the color of the letters on the shirt.

Her head turned towards his before she took off her glasses, placing them on top of her head. She walked over and sat in front of him.

"Where's my little buddy?" she asked.

"With my sister and her son today," he replied and Karmi nodded.

"Did you order already?" Karmi said, pointing at the glass the Marble Slab employees were standing behind.

Langston shook his head. "I want a smoothie."

Karmi ordered a mango smoothie, and Langston got a root beer float. Once they sat back down, Langston figured the conversation was inevitable at the time.

"We're friends, right?" he asked.

Karmi looked up at him and smiled. "As far as I know."

"Well, I need you to be honest with me," he said.

Gauging by the look in her eyes, Langston could tell she was already uncomfortable. She scratched along her jaw line with her left thumbnail and looked around the eatery.

"Be honest about what?"

"The only reason I'm asking is because a few people have questioned it, and I need to know who I have around my daughter."

Karmi sat back against the cream bars that curved to make the back of the chair. She bit her bottom lip before staring directly at him and slowly nodding.

"Did you know Justin and Alisha before we met?" he asked.

Karmi's eyes shined in recognition and a hint of amusement.

"I've seen them a few times."

"Well, both of them seem to question your character based on those few times," Langston said.

He felt as if she was playing games. He didn't want to outright say what he'd assumed. They were in public, and he owed her the benefit of the doubt.

"Well, considering I haven't said possibly more than ten words to each of them, I find that very funny," Karmi replied. "If there is something you feel like you should ask me, then go ahead. We may not have known each other long, but you know I'm an upfront person and you know I wouldn't hurt your daughter. So, make sure you keep that in mind before you delve into my personal life."

She'd said it so quickly that Langston had to sit back a minute and evaluate her statement. She was right in a sense, but that didn't excuse the situation.

"I don't know what's true, which is why I'm coming to you," he said, leaning closer to her over the table so he wouldn't have to speak loud. "They claim to see you leaving different clubs with different men a lot."

"I've had a few."

"Is that something you're proud of?" Langston asked.

"It's something I deal with."

"What does that mean?" he asked, confused.

Karmi frowned as her lips tightened. "The question is why does it matter? I get you wanting to know the people you have around your child. I get that. But, what I do personally does not involve her or you for that matter."

"You're right," Langston said, but that did not diffuse the bomb he'd lit.

"And another thing, Justin and Alisha don't know me. They may see me leaving a club, but that's it. They need to mind their business. I don't have time for this," Karmi said, getting up to leave.

Langston quickly grabbed her hand. She looked at it for a second before sitting back down.

"I don't want you upset. I just wanted to clear it all up," he said.

She sighed before nodding.

"I'm not like that anymore anyway," she mumbled. Langston didn't reply since he wasn't sure how.

The two friends sat in silence as they finished their treats. Langston glanced at her and noticed her eye had completely healed. He wondered if her heart had healed, as well.

The last few months had all been new to him. It was as if Karmi had become another little sister that he felt he needed to look after. She was strong willed, no doubt, but anyone who paid attention could see she was hurting inside.

Langston wouldn't push her to open up to him. She'd do it on her own time.

"We're okay?" Karmi asked.

Langston smiled a little and nodded. "Good. So what's up with you?" she asked.

Langston sighed and proceeded to tell her about his decision to attempt to salvage his family. He knew, of all people, Karmi wouldn't judge.

While writing new chapters into your life, new characters can leap from minor roles to major players. Their importance in your journey can break you down or help you grow. Choosing these characters and their roles is not always entirely up to you. All you can do is go with it and be ready for the lesson this episode brings.

CHAPTER TWENTY-ONE

KARMI

Walking along a bed of bright violets, fuchsias, and emeralds
Time has given her the gift of itself Wandering eyes focused
on the multitude of
warmth coaxing through her body; an outpour through her
eyes deep down into her being Anticipating each touch of
beauty with slender fingers only defusing the fortune instead
Each bright color dimming under her submission, its light
fleeting as she passes
The clinches of her heart hurt from her own wrongdoing;
how she wishes to pull away and stop the pain, yet her
smooth hands continue to crumble the fresh lives along the
way
As the hurt reaches her eyes, she's anticipating her
last step; a desire to lie down and not live is so strong
But, with lightening speed, a flicker of lighted truth reveals
itself ahead with blues, greens, and purples brighter than she
ever thought possible
Thoughts of her terrorist affections conceded Her fear of self-
destruction depleted
She crawls to get there because somehow She just knows

She lay still, twisted at the knees on her couch while various Maxwell songs floated through the air courtesy of the DVD player she had loaded with his albums. It had been a week since she'd revealed to her mother the source of her pain and a few days since Langston questioned her on her past.

Karmi felt transposed.

It wasn't as if the change had come suddenly as she willed herself to believe, but she noticed that ever since she'd stepped foot into Donnica's creative writing class, she'd been changing. However unconscious it may have been at first was beside the point. Writing poetry pulled her away from the need to have sex all the time. When Karmi felt frustrated or depressed, she could write it out instead of scrolling through that fateful list in her phone.

In fact, she had erased all of her contacts.

Karmi smiled at the thought, knowing she hadn't put enough thought into memorizing any of the numbers, just as she hadn't put the thought into remembering their names. At the moment, she was content with her blanket and her notebook.

Some of that contentment washed away when she thought about her mother. She hadn't spoken with her

directly in seven days. An "I love you, too" text message returned only after Karmi had sent three back to back.

But, even with the temporary separation from her mother, Karmi was excited and anxious. Donnica and Amber had sat down with her yesterday, and talks of a poetry collection were on the table. Karmi was sure she would just be a featured author, but Donnica loved her poetry so much that she would have her own collection.

Karmi was floored. She wasn't even a published author, and here they were starting a publishing company on her work alone. Since it was a small press, they had plans for Karmi to appear at a lot of poetry readings and events in Houston and eventually the state. Bigger dreams would soon follow.

It gave her hope, almost a sense of normalcy. She could say things in poetry and twist words around so that only she knew the true meaning, leaving those reading or listening to interpret it any way they needed.

It was the non-judgmental release that she truly needed.

Karmi smirked as she thought of Devin. She was sure he hadn't been published nor had people wanting to start a company off of his work. She thought of waiting until the collection was complete and taking a copy to his church on a night he taught there to rub it in his face. Karmi smiled harder at being able to see the smirk disappear from his face as her credibility rose as well as her confidence.

When her poetry was released, she'd be something more than a sex-crazed woman with suppressed childhood issues. She'd be a published poet.

All in all, her mind was at ease, and the lyrics from the soulful voice slid her further into a bliss that Karmi was positive she'd never be able to reach.

"This has to be what heaven feels like," she spoke aloud. "That and a large sweet cream with a brownie."

Karmi giggled at her silly revelation before wiggling around, pushing her body into the cushions of her couch. She tapped her foot against the armrest, looking at the chipped fingernail polish on her toes in disgust.

An immediate trip to her favorite nail salon disrupted the peace of her afternoon. Her usual spot was sandwiched between a beauty supply store and a personal loan company. There were only a few cars in the yellow spaces, but Karmi hoped they were patrons of other stores and not the nail salon. She hated when she had to sit and wait.

The bell jingled as she pulled open the glass door and welcomed the air-conditioned space. She nodded as the small, round Asian faces glanced up from their current clients to silently acknowledge her. The smallest one sitting near the front nodded before asking Karmi what she needed.

"Pedicure," Karmi stated, pointing down towards her toes that were wiggling between the straps of her thong sandals.

The small Asian said something in her native tongue before one of the women who was sitting by the television got up and went to one of the pedicure chairs.

Karmi watched attentively while the woman cleaned the bowl and rinsed it out. She'd read about women getting infections from nail salons, so she always made sure to pay attention to the cleanliness of the establishment.

The woman soon smiled and motioned Karmi over. It wasn't until her feet were submerged in the hot water that she noticed Devin seated at a station near her while a nail technician gave him a manicure.

Karmi laughed. She'd never seen a man actually get his nails done and wondered why it seemed so foreign to her. He did not look uncomfortable. In fact, he was having a full conversation with the nail tech about her children. It made Karmi laugh louder. Devin looked around for the source of the noise. Karmi thought she saw him roll his eyes before turning back to the nail tech.

"Didn't picture you as a manicure type of guy," Karmi said.

Devin licked his bottom lip and smiled.

"Says the girl who doesn't like judgmental people," he replied, looking back at her.

Karmi's neck strengthened as she frowned and shook her head.

"No, I didn't...I wasn't judging you."

"It's okay," he said. "I like my nails to be neat. No problem in that."

The coolness of how he brushed their misunderstanding off only annoyed Karmi more. She huffed before sitting back in the chair, letting the massage rollers of the chair go over her shoulders before making its way down her spine.

Out of all the nail shops in Houston, she thought. *Why this one?*

Karmi tried to tune him out, except he was the only one in the shop actually talking with the technicians. He'd mentioned his poetry and having gigs at the café Karmi had first heard him in and others around town.

She wondered if it would be like that once her poetry was out. It would be nice to be able to talk to random people and meet new faces on any other basis besides sex.

Karmi closed her eyes and thought about all the poetry she would release to the world. She could feel someone sit down in the chair next to her, and out of curiosity, she opened her eyes and turned to the left.

"Pedicure, too?" Karmi asked, ready for Devin to be out of her space.

"Actually, no," he said, looking at her. "I was wondering if you planned on coming back to hear more poetry."

"I hadn't planned on it after the way you talked to me," Karmi responded.

"I didn't disrespect you." "You judged me."

"You assumed I did," he said. Karmi's nose flared.

"Look, I didn't come over here to get your blood pressure up. I'm just asking a simple question, so stop being so defensive all the time."

"Oh, so you've seen me two times and you've got me figured out, right?" Karmi asked before laughing. "Get over yourself."

"I'd like to see you there again," he said.

His blunt statement shocked Karmi into silence. "Poetry can be healing to anyone."

"So I've heard," Karmi responded.

Devin looked at her a little longer before nodding. He put his hand on the arm of chair, pushing himself up and out of it. He nodded at Karmi and then at the nail tech.

"You enjoy the rest of your day."

Karmi waited until Devin was out of the nail shop to grunt, slamming her back into the chair again.

"You know him?" the nail technician asked with a grin on her face.

"He's just some weirdo," Karmi said, waving him off, but she couldn't shake the feelings of anxiety.

It was almost as if he was still there looking at her through his judging eyes. He ruined her pedicure, which was one of her favorite things.

"Judgmental jerk," she said, before paying for her pedicure and stalking out of the nail salon.

She groaned as the sun hit her face hard, forcing her to pull a pair of brown shades from her purse and put them on quickly. The temperature was heating up, so she knew it was time to go back home.

She made a pit stop for a few groceries, but as she was walking out of the store, she stopped at the bulletin board between the two sets of double doors and perused the ads. A few lost kittens, someone selling puppies, and guitar lessons were plastered all over it. Her eyes stopped on a burgundy flyer, and she soon laughed after reading it. She looked around for a second before pulling the flyer off of the board and walking out of the store. The face that had been haunting her mind looked up at her with details of an upcoming appearance at another jazz café.

Karmi wanted to say she wouldn't go and give him the satisfaction of seeing her there. However, she knew a part of her growth was to stop lying to herself.

He was different that night. His voice was smoother, his outfit more relaxed, and his eyes more confident. Karmi couldn't help but smile when he said something witty or frown in consideration when he said something deep.

His poetry was reading her soul.

She felt like a once popular singer who'd spoken of a performer that captured her essence while performing. The pieces Devin was doing that particular night were different than what she'd heard before.

When he was done, Karmi leaned back against her seat and snapped her fingers quickly. She nodded in approval as he stepped off the stage, knowing now that the trance was broken she could leave before he saw her.

Karmi left a small tip on the table for her waitress and looked for the best possible exit. Just when she thought she was in the clear, a firm grip on her wrist stopped her.

"You're leaving?" he asked.

Karmi looked up at Devin and stepped back a little. She hadn't been that close to a man in a couple of months. Being strong was a work in progress.

"Were you trying to sneak out without me seeing you?" he asked, slightly amused.

Karmi rolled her eyes. "I just love poetry," she said. "Did you love mine?"

Karmi looked around a little before reluctantly nodding. Devin's smile grew.

"I know you may have some type of ill feelings towards me for whatever reason," Devin said.

Karmi began to rebuttal, but he held his hand up and shook his head.

"But, I'm glad you came."

Karmi swallowed the saliva that was gathering in her mouth and slowly nodded. Devin slowly released her wrist and let both of his arms fall to his side.

"I'm really glad you came."

CHAPTER TWENTY-TWO

DONNICA

Reports were in from Afterlight Publishing's first encounter with the media, and it seemed as if Donnica's name appeared more than their company. All of the reporters had mentioned one way or another that she hadn't learned anything from her trouble with Point Set. Some even implied she would be the downfall of this new publishing house.

To say Donnica was furious was an understatement, but she was more hurt and worried. She had put Amber's career in danger before, and she did not want to be the demise of their partnership again. Amber had proved to be a loyal friend and had faith in Donnica's talent.

Donnica would feel horrible if she let her down again, and she was not trying to, but it seemed as if everyone else thought she would.

"Everyone has something to say about me!"

"D, baby, it's the nature of the business," Jeremiah assured her.

Amber nodded. "You can't take it so personal," she said. "This will never work if you do. You want it to work, right?"

Donnica looked up from the dark red binder folded up in front of her to see her husband and business partner staring at her attentively, waiting for an answer. She thought over the question Amber posed and couldn't help but feel the pressure.

"I need it to work."

This wasn't just a dream to her. She'd bet her whole life on writing. Sure, she'd made the mistake of going to college to fulfill her parents' wish, but in the back of her mind, she always remembered her secret reality. When her third grade teacher, Ms. Dooclif, asked her entire class what they wanted to be when they grew up, Donnica said she wanted to be a writer, and in her mind, it was pre- destined.

At that point, she referenced a biblical scripture that she could not truly site, but it was confirmation that even before her birth into the world God had given her a passion for the written word on purpose. This was all no accident.

"Well, we think you'd benefit from an interview coach," Jeremiah said, looking back and forth between Donnica and Amber.

Donnica's face felt hot as Amber agreed. "You two have discussed this?"

"Donnica, you get mad every time someone asks you a question you don't like," Jeremiah continued. "They are going to continue to ask them because they know they can get a rise out of you, and then Afterlight will only be in the media to showcase your anger. Do you want to ruin what you and Amber have worked hard for?"

"No! That's not my intention. It's just…"

Donnica wasn't sure what she could say to explain her actions. Jeremiah caressed her hand from across the table as Amber looked at her with empathy.

She sighed. "If you think it's best."

"It's only two sessions; one coaching and one reviewing," Amber stated.

Donnica nodded, knowing it needed to be done for the sake of their new baby. She'd already had two failed novels, and Donnica didn't want Afterlight Publishing's death on her hands.

Jeremiah lifted her hand to his lips and pressed them to her palm. She smiled before he announced he had another meeting with a different client. Donnica nodded as he left her and Amber alone.

"So what's the next step?" Donnica asked.

"We need to find an editor for the collection and brainstorm some titles."

"Should we bring Karmi in for that?"

"We could, but it might be better to just give her some options to pick from. She's still all new to this," Amber said and Donnica nodded. "We know how important a title and cover can be. We don't want to overwhelm her."

Although Amber was in love with Karmi's poetry, Donnica could tell Amber wasn't totally sold on Karmi as a person. Amber was used to working with seasoned authors who knew how the process worked. However, this was what they had signed up for. Small, independent publishing houses were made for authors like Karmi.

"Just give her a chance, Miss Amber," Donnica said.

"Don't get me wrong, D," Amber replied, shaking her head. "I'm impressed by her lyrical abilities, but I don't know her well enough to be impressed with anything else."

"That's understandable."

"You know I tell it like it is," Amber said, rolling her neck a little, which caused her bangs to slip around her forehead. Her lips were pushed together forming an "o" and her nostrils flared out a little.

Donnica frowned before laughing.

"Was that supposed to be an imitation of me?"

"You could tell, right?" Amber said, laughing. "Means I did you right."

"I guess."

"Well, this meeting is over, darling. Do you have some wine?" Amber asked.

Donnica looked up at her and Amber sighed. "I'm sorry. Are you done with drinking completely?"

"Actually, I am," Donnica responded. She was proud she could say that honestly. "But, there is a bottle left that I haven't gotten rid of yet."

"Well, let me help you out with that," Amber said.

Donnica smiled, telling her where it was stored as Amber walked out of her office and into the kitchen. She leaned back in her chair and tapped her fingernails on the edge of her desk.

Truth was, Donnica had been afraid to even look at the bottle. It seemed so natural to pop open one after a frustrating day or when some reporter misinterpreted her actions. It was even easier to have a celebratory drink or two when goals she had set for herself were checked off of her list.

Donnica realized that for the last few years, she seemed to always have a reason to drink, and she wasn't comfortable with that anymore.

The decisions she would make at this moment in her life were pivotal. Donnica still wasn't sure about an interview coach, but she had heard they did wonders for a lot of others in the entertainment business. She knew the saying "all press is good press", but she didn't want negative connotations when it came to Afterlight, especially if they stemmed from her attitude.

Donnica knew it was time for a serious change and not just to keep talking about it.

It is not always what you wish to hear and it can hurt if your thoughts are far from it, but the truth should always be welcomed in your life. Certain relationships and interactions may not be strong enough to withhold the damage that the truth can do, but once it's all over and you've learned that lesson, you'll be thankful for those around who were honest with you, instead of telling you what you wanted to hear.

CHAPTER TWENTY-THREE

LANGSTON

"Kayla, stop playing and finish counting," Renee said.

"She can take a break," Langston interrupted.

Renee shook her head as Kayla sighed loudly.

"She's going to be the only five-year-old in class who can't count right, and then they're going to talk about my baby. Then she'll grow up to be a social outcast and not have any friends," Renee exaggerated while wailing her arms around for dramatic effect.

"Ugh, Mommy, it's not that serious," Kayla said.

Langston tried not to laugh as Renee stood with both hands on her hips. Kayla sighed again before continuing her counting where she left off at thirty-five.

Langston reached out with his right arm and pulled Renee down on his lap where he sat on the couch. Her body relaxed against his as she pulled the remote out of his hand and flipped through the channels.

"She's not that far behind," Langston whispered into Renee's ear before kissing her cheek.

His chiseled nose pushed past her hair as he inhaled her scent. Renee turned to face him with her pouty lips poked out.

"I know. I just want her to do well in school."

"She will; she's a smart kid."

"With a smart mouth."

"Just like her momma."

Langston laughed as he blocked the small fist coming around to hit him in the chest. Renee folded her leg under his before moving to sit next to him on the couch. Langston looked back down at Kayla, who was diligently writing a list of numbers on a white piece of paper at the coffee table.

It had been five months since Renee and Kayla moved back in with Langston. It had been a decision he wasn't sure about, but seeing Kayla every day was worth it. Renee continued being the redeemed mother, and Langston couldn't even say she was a bad girlfriend. Their work schedules had worked out to where they wouldn't need a sitter unless they wanted time alone, and Kayla was ecstatic to have them both at her beck and call. Of course, she ran the house.

This was the Renee that Langston remembered. The one who loved to play around with their daughter but always took her learning seriously. The one who loved to cook but loved it even more when Langston surprised her with a meal on any particular night. The one he couldn't stand that joked around too much but always seemed to make up for it with the smile that reached her eyes.

It wasn't easy for him to get over the fact that there were no romantic reasons involved in his decision to take her back, but somehow, they were making it work.

"You cooking?" Langston asked, his thoughts of their reunion moving on to matters of substance.

Renee frowned before shaking her head.

"I have a night shift, so we need to order in," Renee replied.

"But Kayla starts school tomorrow."

"I know that. I get off at seven," Renee said.

"She has to be at school by seven forty-five."

"I know we were supposed to get her ready together, but I

laid everything out. All you have to do is get her dressed, and I'll be here to do her hair," Renee told him.

Langston's nostrils flared before he gently pushed her leg off of his.

"L, don't start this mess tonight."

"We were both supposed to call off."

"I tried and they wouldn't let me. What you want me to do, quit?" Renee asked, her voice getting louder.

"Naw," Langston replied, realizing he was overreacting.

Renee rolled her eyes before attempting to move away from him. Langston pulled her back, but she fought against him.

"Let me go. You get on my nerves," she said. He shook his head before kissing her neck.

"No, I don't," he whispered.

She giggled a little before Kayla sighed heavily again.

"You both get on mine."

"I'm about to get on your butt if you keep talking to me that way," Renee said, taking off towards Kayla.

Kayla got up running and giggling while Renee chased her down the hall.

Langston shook his head at two out of five of his favorite women and relaxed into the couch. That was until his phone beeped, letting him know an incoming picture message had downloaded. When he noticed it was from Karmi, he opened it quickly. His eyes had to adjust to the picture, but soon, he recognized it as a book cover of a large quilt with many different pictures in the patchwork. The title was *Blanket Theories: A collection of poetry by Karmi Moore.*

Is this really happening? was the message underneath the picture.

Langston smiled before responding that it was and that he was proud of her. Even though he had read the meat of the collection, to see the finished product would be amazing, especially with knowing how much work Karmi had put into it.

She had become another younger sister to him. He found himself wanting to protect her and help her learn things, but it was usually the other way around. Karmi had a way of looking at things so differently that a lot of people couldn't understand it.

Nobody really understood their relationship except Donnica. Renee was skeptical about any female around that wasn't related by blood; Jus still wasn't satisfied with the fact that Karmi wasn't how she used to be but Kayla still loved her; and Karmi had proven to be a constant support for Langston. She even supported his decision to go back to school. And for that he would always be a loyal friend to her.

"Momma's trying to kill me!" Kayla shouted, running back past the couch and jumping on Langston's lap. "She's trying to tickle me to death."

"You'll remember that next time you talk back then, right?" Langston asked.

He could hear Renee yelling about finding Kayla to tickle her some more.

"Hide me!" Kayla yelled.

Langston repeated his question. "Yes, Daddy, I will. Now help!"

Langston laughed as he threw the blanket that was draped over the couch over Kayla's head. She immediately stopped talking and laid still. Langston carefully laid over her and she giggled.

"Where is that little girl?" Renee said, walking into the living room. She could obviously see where Kayla was hiding.

"I have no idea what you're talking about," Langston said.

Kayla giggled again.

"I think I hear a little girl's giggle," Renee said. "That's just your imagination, baby."

Renee shook her head before smiling. "Well, if you see a little girl that looks like me, tell her when I see her that

it's going down!" "Will do."

Langston waited until Renee walked back into their bedroom before letting Kayla up. She ran her hand over her forehead and sighed, slouching and raising her shoulders.

"Whew, that was a close one."

Langston laughed before kissing her forehead.

The doorbell rang and Renee came out of the back room.

"I hope that's UPS with my package," she said, going for the door.

Langston relaxed back on the couch as Kayla fell into his side to watch television. Langston heard Renee smack her lips and then his brother's voice became audible.

"Move, midget!"

"Don't make me hurt you, Claude," Renee said, turning around and walking away from the door.

Langston could see Jus' nose flare at the call of his first name, but he shook it off.

"When are you going to fire her?" Jus joked, holding his hand out to greet his brother as usual.

Langston laughed.

"Whatever, big head. You know you missed me," Renee said.

"Babe, order a pizza," Langston told her, hoping to intervene before Jus and Renee got out of hand. They had never been the best of friends. Renee nodded and walked into the kitchen.

"Um, hi, Uncle Jus. I know you see me!"

"My bad, beautiful," Jus said, pinching Kayla's nose.

She swatted his hand away and laughed. "Bro, I need a favor."

"No."

Jus threw his hands up as Langston eyed him. He cocked his head to the side and frowned at his big brother.

"Let me finish," he said.

Langston gave him a bored look and he smiled. "I think I'm in love."

"What does that have to do with me?"

"All I want is to chill with my niece for a day," Jus said, causing both Langston and Kayla to look at him.

"What, man?"

"This chick has a little girl, and I kind of promised I'd bring my niece with me to the park tomorrow."

"Hold up. You trying to pimp my child?" Langston asked.

"No. It's not my fault she saw her picture and started talking about how cute she is," Jus said.

"I am cute," Kayla said.

Jus pointed at her and nodded before Langston turned her head towards the television. "Stay out of grown folks' conversations," he told her, then turned his attention back to his brother. "Jus, no."

"You act like I'm going to let something happen to her," Jus said. "Kay, baby, don't you want to chill with Uncle Jus?"

"I'd love to if that trip included a toy or two."

Jus and Langston looked down at Kayla, whose eyes hadn't left the television.

Langston laughed as Jus shook his head.

"My own niece trying to hustle me," Jus said, standing up. "Have her ready by one tomorrow, please."

"If you don't buy her what she wants, I'm going to let her

and Renee jump you," Langston told him.

"Bye, midget!" Jus yelled towards the kitchen.

Renee yelled for him to shut up just as he walked out of the front door.

Our minds can relay information to our hands, instructing the pen of our life to move smoothly and transition to another journey in our lives. We may believe we are doing what needs to be done to ensure the shelf life of our stories, but we soon realize our mistakes. Isn't it great when the ones we tried so hard to replace or remove from the cast don't comply?

CHAPTER TWENTY-FOUR

KARMI

That feeling
That fourth grade, first crush feeling
The one where your stomach turns, your heart flips, and
your toes sweat just at a glance
The teacher asks everyone to introduce themselves and give
a hobby
You're the only girl whose hair is thick and unruly, whose
clothes are an unfamiliar brand,
Whose eyes are a weird mixture of emerald and copper
That feeling of knowing your name isn't simple like Jane or
popular like Tiffany
Yet, you say it with so much pride that the laughter confuses
you
Your throat tightens and you are sure to cry soon But you
look back at him
And he smiles

Karmi sat in her reserved seat, popping the knuckles on her left hand, avoiding her middle finger that had a gold ring on it. She focused on the intricate lines of the temporary henna tattoo she had decided to get the day before during a spur-of-the-moment trip to the spa. The design of flowers, leaves, and vines weaved around her hand. Karmi listened to the woman standing at the podium speak of her recent accolades after recognizing her own name being spoken. In the last few months that *Blanket Theories* had been released, Karmi had listened to many presenters speak as if they knew her personally. Most of the time, Karmi had only met them a few minutes before their thought-out introductions. At first, it was very irritating.

Now it was amusing.

"Her raw and emotional poetry has been the talk of Houston and is quickly growing in popularity. We are so glad that she has joined us for our poet series and would like you all to stand and join me in welcoming Karmi Moore."

The small auditorium at Houston Community College filled with applause and a few even stood to their feet. Karmi exhaled before getting up from her seat, with her book in hand, and walking over to the podium. The long, tan maxi dress she'd worn flowed around her ankles as she adjusted the dark brown belt and straightened her back.

The lights directed at the stage hurt her eyes, and Karmi wished she had her glasses. She learned about unprofessionalism from her first event after a talk with Amber.

"Thank you," Karmi started. "I won't take up too much of your afternoon. I just want to read a few pieces."

She felt like a broken machine as she read the poems that Amber and Donnica thought would sell the collection the best. She almost had them memorized, but kept them with her anyway just in case her mind froze with nerves. With each poem Karmi read, the facial expressions on the faces in front of her changed through a wave of emotions. She had gotten over the initial fear of someone seeing her true self through her work. The audiences she spoke to were too impressed with her talent to worry about if the words were true.

Karmi looked to the right of the stage to see Devin giving her an assuring nod, and she smiled inside. Usually Donnica or Amber made all of Karmi's engagements, but with the success of Afterlight, their schedules were filling up rarely fast. Although she knew Langston would have come to support her, Devin had been asking about her speaking engagements since he purchased *Blanket Theories*.

Karmi always appreciated a familiar face. It helped a lot, especially during the question and answer sessions.

"Small presses are really trending right now, but the larger ones are still holding strong. Do you think you would have more success with a bigger name?"

"I love Afterlight," Karmi replied. "If it hadn't been for them, I wouldn't have even considered being published.

They really took their time and challenged me to look deeper into the source of my poems and make them stronger. I don't know if a larger press with a lot of authors would have given me the same detail."

After a few more questions, Karmi was able to exhale her anxiety and inhale another triumph.

"What were you nervous for?" Devin asked, standing next to her as a few people lined up at the table where an intern from Afterlight was selling Karmi's poetry book, while Karmi sat to sign them. "You did great."

"You're just saying that," Karmi said, not taking her eyes off of the copy in her hand.

"You know me better than that," Devin whispered into her ear.

Karmi blushed a little before trying to focus her attention on the elderly women in front of her who was spelling her name for Karmi to write it.

She looked up to see how many people were in line. It was about four or five left, and she immediately noticed the woman at the end. She was very slim and pale, almost as if she were sick. Her blonde hair was cut short around her ears, but her eyes were very low and bloodshot. The rest of her appearance seemed normal. She wore a pair of denim jeans and a fitted orange short-sleeve shirt with thong sandals to match. However, something about her pulled at Karmi's heart.

Karmi felt anxious waiting for the line to get to her.

Karmi watched her pay for her copy with a few crinkled bills before stepping over in front of Karmi.

"Hey, what's your name?" Karmi asked before the girl could speak.

"Erin."

"Thanks for coming, honey," Karmi said, pulling Erin's copy from her hand and opening it, turning a few pages.

"Thank you. Your poetry inspired me," Erin said. "To tell the truth."

Karmi's pen stopped moving as her eyes connected with Erin's. At that moment, she knew she'd found someone who'd been through a similar situation to hers.

Karmi swallowed the itch in her throat that would surely lead to crying. She then nodded, wrote something, and signed her name. She sighed before kissing the book and handing it back to Erin.

"Are you okay?" Devin asked after he noticed Karmi wasn't moving and everyone was leaving.

"I just never thought it would feel like this," Karmi mumbled. "Knowing someone was inspired by me."

"That's how God works," Devin said, taking Karmi's hand and leading her out of the building. "Our trials become testimonies for others to begin the healing process."

Devin always made uplifting comments to Karmi.

At first, she was a little uncomfortable because she had never really been a religious person. The more she hung out with him and got to know him, though, she realized it was all a part of his appealing character.

Karmi still wasn't sure what it was they were doing.

Donnica often joked that Devin was courting Karmi. He was a perfect gentleman. After a couple of months of them being cordial, Devin confessed his attraction to her. Karmi hadn't been emotionally attracted to anyone in a long time, so it was very different, especially after Devin explained his lifestyle to her.

Devin had been celibate for four years and planned to stay that way until he found his wife. His relationship with God was the only one he'd been in since he'd made his celibacy commitment, and Karmi was scared of that.

Devin took his time to find out everything he could about Karmi that she would allow him to. They had spoken about her molestation, and he'd helped her through the acknowledgment of it now that her relationship with her

mother was strained. He hadn't judged her, but Karmi couldn't bring herself to let him know what that trauma had caused her to do—the men she'd slept with to ease the pain or the relationships she'd possibly ruined, as well.

She didn't want him to look at her differently.

Karmi loved his attention but was terrified at the same time. He was so considerate, yet he challenged her to reciprocity. She was learning a lot about herself from him.

"What are we eating tonight?" Karmi asked.

Devin opened the passenger door to his car and Karmi smiled. He waited until he was comfortably positioned in his seat before kissing her hand.

"No more Mexican," he said.

Karmi laughed before nodding her head. "Well, stop letting me pick the restaurants."

"Maybe I should cook for you tonight."

She couldn't help it. Karmi immediately thought of being alone with Devin in his apartment and felt her skin turn hot. She swallowed hard before she blinked and could almost see her body spread on his bed.

"Let's just grab something really quick," Karmi said.

Devin frowned before pulling off campus. "You don't think I can cook?"

"You probably can't," Karmi joked.

She sighed in relief as Devin changed the subject.

She hadn't wanted to tell him that she didn't trust herself to respect his lifestyle. Karmi had learned ways to get what she wanted from a man sexually, and she didn't want that mindset to slip out while she was with Devin.

Karmi didn't want to ruin him. She had chosen to be the woman she was just as he had chosen to be the man he was. Her feelings for him were growing, and not knowing how to deal with it while he felt so sure was an issue she couldn't handle at the moment.

Her cell phone interrupted the awkwardness, and she silently thanked Donnica for calling.

"How was it?" Donnica asked.

"It was longer than I expected, but we sold quite a few copies," Karmi said.

Donnica always called after an event she couldn't attend to check on Karmi. Even though they were only about seven years apart in age, Karmi looked at Donnica as a mother figure in her newfound career. She had guided Karmi to something she never knew she wanted until she got it.

"That's great. Are you ready for the trip this weekend? We leave for New York a little before noon."

"I'm nervous but ready," Karmi replied.

This would be her first trip out of state, and the writer's conference in New York made her anxious about it. It was more of a workshop for small presses, but there would be an opportunity to showcase Karmi's poetry collection. So, Donnica and Amber wanted her to come along.

"Well, I'll call you within the next day or so to give more details."

"Thanks."

"I can't believe you're leaving me for a week," Devin said after she ended the call.

Karmi smiled at his playful tone of sadness. "You're a big boy. You can handle it."

Devin glanced at her while pulling up to a local chicken restaurant.

"It's not that I can't," he said, gently caressing her hand. "It's that I don't want to."

Karmi looked into his eyes and saw how sincere he was. She had the urge to push his car door open and run for her life, but she sat frozen by his glance. Falling for someone was one of the scariest things Karmi could ever think to do.

At this point, though, she couldn't stop herself even if she tried.

CHAPTER TWENTY-FIVE

DONNICA

Donnica's smile reached up to the corners of her eyes as she tilted her head slightly to the right. Her fresh auburn highlights glinted in the lighting around her. She nodded as Cathy, the woman interviewing her for a local television station, talked.

They were inside a small meeting room in the building that had a long conference table with black leather rolling chairs on both sides. There was a square backdrop with an abstract painting hanging on it, a single chair, and a faux plant in the corner. The lighting was set up once Donnica sat down, while Cathy sat next to the camera off screen.

"First of all, congratulations on the success of *Blanket Theories*," Cathy said.

"Thank you!" Donnica started. "Karmi is such a talented poet, but the collection is surpassing our expectations. It's a blessing."

"Speaking of expectations, we asked Steve Point how he felt about Afterlight," Cathy said. "For my viewers who don't know, Steve Point is the founder of Point Set Publishing. Last year, Donnica and her partner Amber Coley were both with

Point Set, but after an unfortunate turn of events, they left out on their own. Donnica, how have you redeemed yourself from your violent exit from that company?"

"I was very emotional when released from Point Set. The stress of my novels not selling and being let go just kind of broke me at that point," Donnica said, looking at the camera. "I've wanted to write ever since I was a little girl, and it was a harsh reality to face that I wasn't succeeding at it. Everything kind of spiraled to a point where I had to stop, look at myself, and ask what behaviors and attitudes were causing this negative vibe in my life. I got rid of them and moved on."

"Good for you," Cathy said. "We all have to fall and get back up."

"Or the fall wouldn't be worth it," Donnica added. Cathy looked at her and smiled before nodding. "So what's next for Afterlight?" Cathy inquired.

"We are excited about a new novelist we are working with, and we are also working on Karmi's next poetry collection. She writes like a machine."

Both women laughed as Donnica licked her bottom lip and crossed her legs at her ankles.

"That's great. That's just awesome," Cathy said. "Well, we look forward to hearing more from you guys."

"Thank you so much," Donnica said. "Thanks for having me."

The camera cut, and Donnica thanked Cathy again before walking off set. Amber stood there shaking her head. She didn't come on camera because of a cold but refused to not be on set. Her hair was pulled up into a messy bun, and her casual clothes consisted of a gray and dark pink tracksuit and sneakers. If she weren't sick, Donnica would have teased her about it.

"That was almost scary," Amber said, while Donnica smiled. "That interview coach changed you," she joked.

Donnica laughed before pushing Amber away. "Don't get me sick," she said. "We have more interviews."

"Which you are killing!" Amber said. Donnica smiled at her excitement.

"These reporters are so mad that they can't get you to bite anymore."

"I know. I shouldn't have let them get hype about it in the first place."

"Well, all that matters is that Afterlight is a growing business and we are well on our way, missy," Amber told her.

Donnica stood true to her word and had two sessions with an interview coach. He taught her ways to work around the questions that a lot of reporters posed about her bad habits. He challenged her to talk about her emotions at the point of those bad habits without actually mentioning her actions and then about how much she had grown. Lastly, but the most important information he could give Donnica, point the direction of the conversation back to Afterlight Publishing.

Placing her hand under her chest and exhaling, she idly wondered if she could stay as poised in the future.

"Yes, that's all that matters."

Three interviews and four hours later, Donnica was entering the combination to turn off her home alarm. She was glad Jeremiah wasn't home yet. It gave her time to think.

Donnica hadn't been prepared for the turn of events her life had taken. When her marriage was strained and her career was fading, she never knew things could change so much in a year. Donnica worked hard to regain control of her life, but an unexpected pregnancy had changed all that immediately.

How unexpected it was, Donnica wasn't sure. She hadn't been on any type of contraception since she and Jeremiah separated, and it was not on either of their minds once reunited. They had discussed kids years ago before they were married and never made a decision to go either way. Once both of their careers bloomed, there was no need to discuss it.

They hadn't been back together for an entire year, and here she was about to change their lives again. Donnica just knew this wouldn't go like it did in the movies, so for now, she would keep it to herself.

Having discovered that the hormonal imbalance she was going through at just eight weeks weighed heavily on her sleeping patterns, Donnica decided to take a nap before preparing dinner. She awoke to the sun going down and her cell phone vibrating against the coffee table. She had a message from Jeremiah saying new evidence was found on a case and he would be working late, but the other message from Karmi made Donnica return her call immediately.

"Are you busy?" Karmi asked, not even giving Donnica a proper greeting. "Can I stop by?"

"Sure. Is everything okay?" "I'll tell you once I get there."

Donnica examined her living room to make sure nothing was too out of place and then ordered a sausage and pineapple pizza, a side of hot wings, and breadsticks.

Karmi arrived just after the pizza did.

"You look like you've been crying," Donnica said, pulling Karmi into the house.

Karmi nodded before scratching her temple with her left hand and looking around.

"Jeremiah's not here, is he?" she asked.

"No, he's still at work. Come on, tell me what's wrong."

"I'm freaking out, D."

They went into the kitchen, the smell of the pizza almost distracting Donnica from the worry of what was wrong with Karmi. She inwardly groaned after opening the box to see the cheese oozing off the sides of the dough. She turned the box to Karmi, who shook her head no, before pulling a slice up for herself.

"What's wrong? Did something happen with your mom?"

"Devin told me that he loved me."

"Awww," Donnica said, tears immediately filling her eyes.

Karmi frowned at her before her nose flared a little. "Are you about to cry?"

Donnica waved her off and fought the tears back. "What's the problem?"

"I'm not ready for this. We've only known each other for six months!" Karmi explained. "I'm just now getting used to the idea of dating without any physical contact. I'm just getting used to the idea of dating period!"

Donnica nodded in understanding so that Karmi would know she was paying attention while she ate.

"What did you do when he said it?"

"Luckily, we were on the phone. So, I hung up and acted like I didn't hear him."

Donnica looked at Karmi skeptically and she nodded.

"I'm serious, D."

"You ought to be ashamed," Donnica said.

Karmi threw her hands up in surrender. "What else was I supposed to do?"

"Explain to him what you just said to me and probably why you feel that way."

"Sure, I'll tell him, 'Devin, I can't love you because I'm not even sure what that means considering I'm a recovering sex addict'."

"Some men like the experience," Donnica joked.

"Donnica, be serious! Devin has been celibate for the longest," Karmi said. "I'd probably scare him off. I'm scared to even touch him."

"It's your first real relationship, honey," Donnica said, pulling meat off of a wing. "Give yourself time."

"I want him bad," Karmi admitted. "I can't ruin him."

No matter how hard Donnica tried to convince Karmi to just tell Devin how she felt, she resisted. Donnica knew Karmi liked the way Devin thought of her without the judgment of her past.

"Sometimes, though, for the sake of your future, you have to take that chance," Donnica said.

A tear fell from Karmi's eye as she shook her head.

The chapters we recreate for our own story often etch the outline of someone else's. We focus on the rebirth of our tale before we submit those ideas to others, wanting to be accepted and published in their lives. We love how they read our thoughts with enthusiasm and excitement, but when confusion on past chapters comes into question, we stop writing and wish for an internal delete.

CHAPTER TWENTY-SIX

LANGSTON

Langston pushed the door open to Marble Slab and immediately saw Karmi in line ordering.

"Kar!" Kayla yelled, running over to her.

Karmi turned with a smile before lifting Kayla up in her arms. Langston rolled his eyes, walking over to them.

"I told you about picking her up," Langston said. Karmi frowned before putting her down.

"You shouldn't have had such a cute kid," Karmi replied, ordering for all three of them.

They found a booth in the front and sat down, Langston on one side and Karmi and Kayla on the other.

"You bring the books?" Langston asked.

Karmi nodded. "You needed two, right?" "Yep, one for Mom and one for Jessie."

"You know you don't have to pay for them, right?"

"I know I do," Langston said, already counting out three ten-dollar-bills from his wallet. "What type of friend would I be if I always asked for free things?"

"A normal one."

Karmi laughed, but Langston just shook his head, pushing

the money over on the smooth tabletop towards her. Karmi pulled two copies of her poetry collection from her oversized purse and did the same.

"I signed them already."

"How does it feel to be a superstar?" Langston asked.

Karmi shrugged. "I've got other issues to worry about," she said.

Langston looked at her to continue, but she glanced at Kayla uncomfortably.

"You remember Devin?"

"How could I forget him?" Langston teased.

Karmi talked about him a lot. When she caught on to his joke, she threw a napkin at him.

"What's up with him?" he asked.

"Well, remember that thing I said he doesn't do?" Karmi continued, looking down at her ice cream and shaking her head.

Langston frowned when he saw a tear fall from her eye.

"I thought you agreed to respect it?" he asked. Karmi violently shook her head before wiping the tear away.

"I had every intention of doing so. Now I feel horrible. I feel worse than horrible."

Langston wasn't sure what to say to her. He was skeptical of a man being celibate. He'd heard some men used that as a game to get women, but after about the third or fourth month, Langston realized Devin was serious. He couldn't lie and say he wasn't disappointed in Karmi, but she was beating herself up about it enough.

"Say something to make me feel better about this," Karmi pleaded.

Langston shook his head. "You need to talk to him and figure out what it is that happens next," he said.

"I haven't spoken to him since," Karmi mumbled. Langston

sat up straight and gave her a stern look.

Kayla was too into her ice cream to notice the change in the atmosphere.

"He's probably thinking you used him."

"I know, but I just can't face him."

"Karmi, you need to grow up," Langston said. Karmi's eyes shot daggers through him.

"Excuse me?"

"How long are you going to hide behind your past?" he asked.

Karmi looked down at her ice cream and shrugged her shoulders.

"You at least owe him an explanation."

"I know," Karmi said, "but it's not one that I want to give."

It was Friday. Langston couldn't stop smiling as he walked through the exit of his job with his head high. He nodded to a few co-workers as he passed, glad his work shift was over. Not only was it Friday, but also Langston had just been promoted to manager, which meant he had weekends off.

It was time to celebrate and what better way to do that than with family. He would go straight to his sister's house since he knew Renee and Kayla got there about an hour ago.

Everything about his day was perfect. He hadn't faced too much traffic after getting off work, and the weather wasn't as harsh as usual. When he got to his sister's and noticed all of the cars, he knew his good day would continue thanks to his family.

Langston laughed as he watched Kayla and his nephew Ashton run around Renee. It was Ashton's birthday, and Ryan and Jessie decided to have a small family get-together in their backyard instead of going all out. Ashton was six now and seemed to be getting taller every time Langston saw him.

Kayla conned Renee into playing musical chairs with them,

and it was hilarious to watch.

"I always knew I liked her," Jessie said, as Ryan, Jus, and Langston all looked at her in shock. "What?"

"Quit lying!" Jus said. Ryan laughed and Langston just shook his head. "You couldn't stand her," Jus added.

"I never said that," Jessie said, pushing her back into the lawn chair and rolling her eyes.

"You never had to, child."

Langston smiled at his mother as she walked through the sliding door onto the porch. A sober look played against Jessie's features. Langston knew she wouldn't go against what their mother said. She never did.

"Miss Henrietta, you remembered the cake, right?" Ryan asked.

Their mom rolled her eyes before looking back at her son-in-law.

"Don't ask me that again, Ryan. It's on the dining room table."

Jus laughed at the look on his sister's face and shook his head, taking a swig of his beer.

"Now when are you going to get married and have some kids?" Miss Henrietta asked.

Jus looked at her and frowned. "L ain't married, Momma."

"Might as well be," Jessie chimed in.

"I was talking to you Claude Justin," she said.

Jus groaned. "No time soon." "Well, work on that."

Langston smiled and sat back, watching his family interact. He always laughed hard with them, especially around his mother. She was so blunt and raw that you couldn't help but be entertained. That was until her bluntness was pointed towards you.

Langston watched Renee pop up out of her chair and chase

after the kids. They all took off running, screaming and flailing their arms around in laughter.

He thought about his friend Karmi and the predicament she was in at the moment. It made him appreciate Renee a little more.

"Kayla, Mommy hit her toe," Renee said, slowing down and sitting in the middle of the yard. She pushed her flip-flop off and crossed her right leg at the knee to get a better look. "I quit."

"I'm sorry, Mommy. I ran too fast, huh?" Kayla asked, circling around her and waving her arms at her side. She huffed a few times before finally stopping in front of Renee.

"You did," Renee said. "You're like lightning, girl."

"How so?"

"Lightning moves really, really fast!"

"Yes!" Kayla said, her eyes bright. "I'm lightning!"

Renee laughed a little before squeezing her big toe to relieve the pain.

"You want me to kiss it?" Kayla asked.

Renee frowned. "No, but you can kiss right here," she said, pointing to her cheek and turning sideways.

Kayla smiled and kissed Renee on her cheek before running to catch up with her cousin and the other kids.

Langston smiled as he got up and walked over to Renee, holding both of his hands out to her.

Sure, she had put him through a lot and pushed all of her responsibilities off on him. However, she'd come back around not only because she wanted a relationship with her daughter, but Renee wanted one with Langston, too.

"I can't believe she offered to kiss your foot," Langston said, helping Renee up.

She looked up at him and grinned. "Don't act like you haven't before."

"Hey, that's something you don't need to be saying out loud," he said, looking around the yard.

Renee laughed before trying to move. Langston held on to her hips tighter and she looked back up at him.

"What?"

"Nothing," Langston said but continued to stare at her. Renee bit her lip and shifted her weight to her left leg.

"Stop acting nervous."

"Stop acting like a stalker."

Langston laughed before placing his lips against her forehead and then letting her go. Renee winked at him and then went back towards the house after his mother called her over.

He wasn't sure how he'd feel if he were in Devin's shoes with Karmi, but he thanked God that he didn't have to be.

Your past entries can often dictate how you view new chapters in your life. You may often want to revert back to a past habit that made you feel safe and secure. Those habits can be familiar and comforting, and it may be a place for you to rethink your next move. However, staying in the past does not help rewrite your future.

CHAPTER TWENTY-SEVEN

KARMI

The greatest tasting dessert that I never knew I wanted
Better than sweet cream with brownies, better than hot fudge
and caramel dripping from my fingers Your aroma covers
every inch of me; I love how your smell lingers
A child wanting to skip to the good part So tempted to
indulge before dinnertime
Your preparation was divine from the start I could not wait
until you were mine

It was strenuous now for Karmi to do everyday things that had become second nature to her. She couldn't make her bed, brush her teeth, or fix her breakfast without thinking about Devin. The guilt of what she'd done was taking over her life, especially since he'd stopped calling.

It had been three weeks since Karmi jumped out of Devin's bed while he was sleeping as if a fire had lit her entire body. She wasn't proud of her actions after the fact, but what could she do besides ignore him and hope he would go away?

He had stopped calling four days ago, and Karmi couldn't be more depressed about it.

The morning after they slept together, Devin had been

calling, sending texts and emails, trying to assure Karmi it wasn't all her fault. He had a part in it, giving into the temptation he'd felt for months, but Karmi wasn't convinced. After all, she was that temptation.

She felt horrible. She never cried about the actual act of sex before, but Karmi knew everything about that was wrong. Being around Devin had changed her subconsciously. She had always been about doing what felt good, but now, she was hurting. It hurt to know she'd made him compromise something he felt so strongly about.

Yet, no part of her would allow her to say it wasn't the most satisfying feeling, having sex with someone who cared about her. That night played like a movie in her head all the time.

Karmi sighed as the comfort of Devin's apartment overtook her body. She'd been at work only five hours, but having taken a week off for promotion of her poetry book, she wasn't used to it. Everything inside of her wanted to quit, but the money from Blanket Theories *wasn't as stable as her bi-weekly checks from the department store.*

Karmi had been avoiding going to Devin's place for the last few days. She hated that the cliché 'old habits die hard' was true. She was itching to be intimate with him.

It made her ashamed when she thought about it. She was twenty-two years old. How was she not able to have a close relationship without sex? Karmi thought only guys had that problem.

"Hey, beautiful," Devin said, giving Karmi a quick kiss on her lips. The fire started. "You tired?"

"As I look," she responded, kicking her flat dress shoes off by the door, scooting them to the corner with her left foot.

She looked up to see Devin's back disappearing into the kitchen. Visions of pushing him into the wall or hopping on the counter crossed her mind. She shook her head and went into the living room instead of following him.

"Well, I know you said you ate on your break, but I bought you ice cream," he said from a distance.

Karmi smiled as she slid down on the couch and sunk into the pillows. *He's too sweet,* she thought.

"Thanks, Dev," she said aloud as she closed her eyes.

"Did anyone come up to you about the book?" Devin asked.

Karmi could hear his voice getting closer. She turned to see him coming towards her with a small Marble Slab container and a spoon.

"No," she said. "I usually don't get recognized unless I'm in a bookstore or something."

That part was cool to Karmi. She'd never heard of authors being stalked like celebrities. The only time she had to worry about it was when she was on an actual interview or a book signing or event. She could always relax and be herself most of the time.

The weight on the couch shifted as Devin sat next to Karmi. Feeling his body heat, she tensed up. Devin reached over and kissed her forehead before handing her the ice cream and grabbing the remote.

She snuggled next to him and ate her ice cream while he watched ESPN. She loved that he was comfortable with her now. When they first began to get close, he'd rather not sit this close to her.

It made Karmi wonder what else he would allow. They never really talked about his celibacy, and although she had admitted to Donnica that she didn't want to taint him, the thought was becoming more and more desirable.

Their similar heights gave Karmi the advantage of being able to examine his profile without straining or making it obvious that she was checking him out. He had recently gotten a fade and a line up; Karmi could tell because the edges of his beard were perfect. Her mouth watered just a little as her eyes glazed over his smooth, milk chocolate skin. She felt like running away from him as he laughed at something said on the television. When he laughed was when Karmi felt it the most. His brown eyes would light up and that small gap she loved would become visible.

"I should go home," she whispered to herself, yet she leaned a little closer to Devin.

"Huh?" he asked.

Karmi shook her head. "I didn't say anything."

Her voice was shaky. She knew it because he turned to her with a concerned face.

"You okay?"

Karmi bit her lip and nodded, surrendering to the power in his eyes. He smiled at her before leaning down to kiss her.

Now was her chance.

She pressed her lips harder into his and was rewarded with a groan. Her tongue burned for attention, and to her surprise, when she parted her lips and pushed it against Devin's bottom lip, he accepted.

Karmi gripped his right shoulder with her left hand, afraid that he'd pull away at any moment. Her mind wanted desperately to let him go, but she couldn't. When his arm went around her waist, Karmi pushed her breasts into his chest. A moan escaped her lips and that was when he pulled back.

She reached for him again, stronger this time. Both of her arms wrapped around his neck as she pushed her lips back to his. In just that short period of time, Karmi decided she needed to kiss him like this all the time now.

"You need to chill," he groaned, opening his palms against her side in an attempt to push her back, but he never did.

"No," Karmi whined.

Just as she was about to press her luck and straddle his lap, Devin sighed and pushed her away. Karmi frowned from the pressure on her stomach, but her heart dropped when he stood up and walked away.

She sat on his couch trying to catch her breath and calm her body. Hoping to recall any coping method that Dr. Reynolds had taught her, Karmi closed her eyes as her legs bounced against the couch. The fire in the pit of her stomach had been lit, and there was nothing she could do about it.

The only thing to do now was satisfy it.

Karmi racked her brain, knowing it had to be done soon.

She idly thought of calling someone but remembered she'd erased all of her contacts as a healing process in therapy. She wouldn't have time to go to a club. She didn't want to anyway. She wanted Devin.

Karmi turned to look towards the hallway. No lights were on. She slowly rose from the couch and took small steps, hoping not to disturb the stillness of his place. She stopped once she got to the frame of his bedroom door. Her right hand stopped her from going in, holding on to the frame, yet her body leaned forward. Devin was seated on the opposite side of his bed with his back to the door. His elbows rested on his knees and his head was down.

Karmi walked around slowly and stopped once she was inches in front of him. He didn't look up. She swallowed the saliva around her tongue while gripping the edge of her work shirt with both

hands, crossing her arms and pulling upward.
   The shirt hit the floor with a soft thud. Devin still didn't look up.
Karmi's heart thumped in her chest as she unbuttoned her black
   slacks, pushed the zipper down, and let them fall to the ground.
She kicked the pants out in front of her, right between his legs.
   Devin's head began to rise slowly. Karmi waited patiently until
they met her own. He bit his lip as she moved closer. Placing her
hands on his shoulders, Karmi straddled his lap.
   This time, Devin didn't protest.

She was grateful the success of the poetry collection had allowed her to drop down to working part-time at the department store. She would take the day to try and ease her mind, and she knew the only person who could was Neiva.

It wasn't easy trying to rebuild their relationship. Karmi knew it wasn't an option not to. She wished she'd never told Neiva about what happened with Hassun years ago. It hadn't helped. Dr. Reynolds was wrong.

Neiva and Karmi weren't the same, but an understanding had been formed that neither of them would discuss it. However, deep down somewhere in her soul, Karmi was hurt by Neiva's reaction. Karmi had gone over and over in her head how she thought that conversation would go, and the reality of it still was never a possibility.

After going to Donnica and Langston about the situation, Karmi realized she had nowhere else to turn except to her mother.

Her mother's home seemed different. It held the same comforting tone, but it didn't calm Karmi's nerves at all. She could hear her mother's favorite talk show from the kitchen television after using her key to enter.

"Neiva?" Karmi called out.

The volume was lowered a little and she called her name again, knowing that sometimes Neiva's mind got the best of her.

"In the kitchen."

Pushing her purse onto the marble counter near the door, Karmi smiled upon seeing her mother for the first time in a couple of weeks. Neiva stood from the table just as Karmi removed her sunglasses from her eyes and placed them on top of her head in front of her bun.

"You've gotten used to this hairdo," Neiva said, patting the back of Karmi's head before wrapping her arms around her.

"How are you?" Karmi asked.

"I'm moving," she said. "Got a job down at the school around the corner." Neiva looked up at Karmi for a moment before letting her go and walking back over to the table.

"A job?" Karmi asked. "Why?"

When Karmi's father died, because of the insurance policy, his job, and his savings, Neiva didn't need to work. She kept a pretty modest life, and Karmi never thought she'd work again.

"I got bored."

Karmi shrugged at her response before sitting across from her to see what she was doing. Neiva had been looking through an old scrapbook of Karmi and her father on a fishing trip. It reminded Karmi that she hadn't been fishing in a while. She used to love to go.

"Anyway, it's sort of a teacher's assistant type of position," Neiva continued. "I only work a few hours a day. The English teacher there loves your poetry. She asked for an autographed copy."

Karmi nodded absentmindedly. Neiva pushed the open book over to her, and she began to flip through the pages.

On one page, her father had driven to Galveston, even though Neiva hated for him to go. She always complained about how dirty and matted Karmi's hair was when they came back because of how nasty the water was, but he would usually just kiss her and ignore her complaints. Karmi always thought it was funny how they interacted together.

In the first picture, they were seated on the dock waiting for their rental to get ready. Karmi had her head on her father's shoulder with her eyes closed, and he was looking out at the water.

She'd love to have that picture framed in her apartment.

"I spoke with Devin yesterday," Neiva said. "He's asking for some of that soup I made him last time he was over here. That man is very nice. I like him."

Karmi nodded as she flipped the page but stopped once it got mid-air. She slowly turned to look at Neiva, who was busy rearranging the salt and pepper shakers in the middle of the table.

"You...you spoke with Devin?"

"I just said that, child," Neiva said, getting up and rummaging around the kitchen.

Karmi closed the scrapbook and turned in her chair. "What else did he say?"

"That he hadn't spoken to you in a few days.

You've both been very busy." Now Karmi was confused.

"Karmiti, why don't you call him and tell him to come over? He doesn't stay too far from here."

"Mommy, he's probably busy." "Call and see."

Before getting up to get her cell phone from her purse, Karmi eyed her mother to see if anything was suspicious about her behavior. She then walked into the living room and plopped down on the couch to call Devin. To her surprise, he answered.

"Um, you spoke with my mom the other day?" she asked, not sure what else to say. "Is that a crime?"

"No, no. I'm just here now and she wants to see you,"

Karmi replied. "But, I can tell her that you're busy."

"I don't mind coming over to see her," Devin said. Karmi's heart softened at hearing his voice.

"However, I'd rather discuss some things in private with you first."

The lump in her throat fought its way back down before she nodded.

"I just got here, though."

"We can just take a quick drive and I'll bring you back."

Before hanging up, Karmi told him yes and then went to relay the information to her mother.

Devin arrived at Neiva's house in no time. Karmi left her things inside to assure Neiva of their return and walked slowly out to Devin's car. Karmi knew from his facial expression that he wasn't happy with her. Yet, he got out of the car to open her door.

He started driving in silence.

"I know you're upset," Karmi started, but he cut her off.

"Not for why you think I am."

"I was wrong. I initiated it all and I'm sorry," Karmi said, trying to keep her tears at bay.

Devin pulled over, parked the car, and turned to face her.

"Stop it."

"What?"

"Stop feeling sorry about the situation. It happened and we need to move on from it. Did you pray about it?"

Devin's question caught Karmi off guard, but she slowly nodded because she had. She wasn't sure if she'd done it right, but she had.

"I want to be with you," he said.

"Still?" she asked, wondering how he could possibly still be interested in her life's mess.

"Still," he replied, grabbing her hand and kissing it, causing

Karmi to blush. "We just have to do this the right way."

Once their drive ended, Devin drove back to Neiva's house and followed Karmi inside. Neiva was in the middle of making a pie to go with her homemade ice cream.

"How'd you make it that fast?" Karmi asked, looking through the small glass of the oven window.

"You've been gone awhile," she said. "Devin, do you eat cherry pie?"

"I'll try it," he said.

Neiva nodded before sitting down. "So tell me about this celibacy thing. How does it work?"

"Mommy!" Karmi said, shocked at her mother's boldness.

Devin held his hand up and smiled.

"It's okay," he said. "People do it for a lot of different reasons. Once my relationship with God grew stronger, I realized it was the right thing to do until I find my wife."

"And you've never thought someone was the one before?" Neiva asked.

Devin looked up at Karmi and shook his head. "The women I've been with have either run away because of it or tried to deal with it and ended up backing away. It hasn't been easy."

I tried to run, Karmi thought, immediately feeling ashamed. She hadn't considered how Devin felt in the situation, only about how she'd felt.

"So how long are you willing to wait?" "As long as it takes."

"Mommy, why don't you go check on the pie?" Karmi asked. Devin looked at her and smiled as Neiva got up. "She's so embarrassing."

"She's not that bad."

Karmi shook her head, running her left hand down her face. When she opened her eyes, Devin's face was a little closer to hers.

"You are beautiful," he said. "I love you." "I don't deserve a man as good as you," she
whispered.

"I've waited a long time for you," Devin continued, ignoring her statement. "I want you to be my wife."

Karmi felt her senses shut down as she swayed a little in the chair. She looked down between the two of them to see Devin holding a white gold sapphire and diamond ring between his left thumb and index finger. Tears fell from her eyes as he took his right hand and lifted her face level with his.

"I thought I'd lost you," she admitted. "I was giving you space."

"Is this because of what happened?" she asked. He shook his head in the negative.

"It's because I know in my heart you're the one I've been waiting for. Although you came in the most beautiful, unconventional, shocking and, in the beginning, rude package I could have expected, I know."

Karmi laughed through her tears before attempting to smile.

"Can we take that as a yes?" Neiva asked from behind them, peering over towards the table from the counter.

Karmi laughed before nodding her head.

CHAPTER TWENTY-EIGHT

DONNICA

Donnica rushed through her home making sure everything was in place as some of her guests began to arrive. She hadn't wanted to go overboard with her decorations, so she settled on a modest champagne color to complement the colors of her home. Although Neiva wanted to cook most of the food, Karmi had talked her into letting them hire a caterer so Neiva could enjoy the day.

She thanked God for the weather, only hitting a high of eighty-five that day, because most of her backyard was set up for this wonderful occasion.

Once Karmi called Donnica with the good news, she knew she wanted to throw an engagement party for the couple. Karmi was against it, still not used to all of the attention being on her. However, it didn't take long for Donnica to convince Devin and Neiva that it was a good idea. So, ultimately, Karmi was outvoted. She made the party modest since she knew Karmi wasn't much of a people person. Most of Devin's family was there and associates of Afterlight showed up to support. Donnica was even surprised to see Langton from the creative writing class, but soon found out he and Karmi had become close friends. He brought along his girlfriend, as well.

She decorated the bathroom and the foyer all the way to the patio doors just to stay along with the theme. She didn't plan on anyone walking around her home, but she cleaned every room anyway. There were several round tables and lawn chairs with champagne-colored draping and one rectangular table that held the food. The caterers were set up in the kitchen and prepared to cook as much food as needed during the event.

Donnica loved doing things like this, knowing event planning would have been her fall back if she hadn't ventured out into the publishing world.

She rounded the corner from the kitchen to the living room, and her heart jumped a little as Jeremiah caught her.

"Slow down and kiss me, wife," he said.

Donnica covered her mouth as he leaned in towards her. Jeremiah frowned.

"I just sampled the garlic shrimp, baby," she said, stepping back. "I'll be right back."

Donnica rushed upstairs, sure that Jeremiah was watching her. She knew he didn't care she'd eaten something that may have tarnished her breath. Truth was morning sickness had kicked in. Since her pregnancy would be hidden until later that evening, food was her only alibi to explain the nasty taste in her mouth.

Donnica rushed into the bathroom and grabbed the mouthwash sitting on the granite counter. She sipped it carefully, not wanting anything to drop on her silk maxi dress, and stood eyeing herself in the mirror as she swished it around in her mouth.

The minty taste of the mouthwash made her stomach turn. She closed her eyes and took small breaths through her nose before spitting it out in the sink.

Donnica slid past her office door but looked into it after noticing it was open. She poked her head inside and smiled upon seeing Karmi looking up at a book on the shelf.

"This party is for you, you know?" Donnica joked.

Karmi turned around quickly, but her features softened at recognition of her mentor.

"More like for Devin and Neiva," Karmi replied with a smirk.

"What are you in here thinking about?"

"What did you do after *No Spaces* was released?" Karmi asked.

Donnica bit her lip in thought. She smiled before sitting on the edge of her desk, placing both hands in her lap near her belly.

"Well, the very first thing I did was run to Jeremiah's campus apartment and woke up the entire floor with my cries," she said.

They both laughed.

"But, then I began to wonder what was next."

Karmi nodded while scratching the inside of her bun with her index finger. She was thinking that exact thing.

"What do I do?" Karmi asked.

"You keep writing," Donnica answered. "If that's what you want to do."

"More poetry?" "Whatever you want."

Donnica felt peace from looking at the hopeful gleam in Karmi's eyes. It was a mound of untold stories in them, and Donnica felt right in her literary world having discovered Karmi. She vowed to help her in any way she could.

"I'm ready for this to be over," Karmi admitted.

"Well, I have a bit of news that can take a little of the attention off of you, if you don't mind."

"I don't, especially since you tricked me into this party anyway," Karmi pointed out while eyeing Donnica, who smirked as someone came in the door.

"I know you're hiding from everyone else, but I'll need you

not to hide from me," Devin said as he walked in.

Karmi smiled before reaching out for him. "People are starting to get antsy," he told them. "Guess now is as good a time as any."

Karmi sighed, biting her lip as Devin interlaced their fingers and walked out of the room behind Donnica. They passed through the kitchen and out into the backyard where glasses of champagne were being passed around and smooth jazz flowed from the speaker set up near the door. Donnica smiled in approval as she walked over to Jeremiah.

"Hey, beautiful," he said, kissing her forehead. She smiled before grabbing his hand.

"I have an announcement to make," she said. "But, I want to tell you in private first."

"Is this going to make me upset or happy?" he asked after Donnica pulled them into their unoccupied living room.

She bit her bottom lip and arched her eyebrows.

"It all depends on how you feel about being a dad," she responded, her shoulders hunched to emphasize her question.

She could feel Jeremiah's hands tense in hers as a mixture of emotions displayed across his face.

"Are you…are you pregnant?" he asked.

With her teeth still holding firm to her bottom lip, she nodded slowly. Donnica released the air she had been holding as Jeremiah's grin grew into a smile.

"So far, all I know is that I'm about eleven weeks. I found out a few weeks ago."

Jeremiah frowned. "Why are you just now telling me?"

"I don't know. I was nervous about all this and we just got back together and we're getting our flow back and…" Donnica began to ramble.

Jeremiah sighed before pulling her body into his. Donnica allowed herself to relax a little before he pulled away.

"Don't keep something like this from me again," he said, looking into her eyes.

Donnica nodded before receiving a kiss.

"So are you excited about being a dad?" Donnica asked.

Jeremiah kissed her again while cupping her face with both of his hands. "I'm excited about being a family."

Donnica giggled when Jeremiah's hands rounded her belly and he mentioned not being able to wait until she was truly showing. She pushed his hands off before telling him that she owed Karmi a favor, and they both headed back outside.

Karmi was at the door waiting. "Please save me," she whispered through a tight smile.

Donnica laughed and then asked Jeremiah to pause the music. Soon, all eyes were on them.

"I just want to thank you all for coming out to celebrate the engagement of Karmi and Devin," she said, giving everyone a chance to settle down. She looked at Karmi and sighed. "This woman, although a few years younger than me, has been a much-needed inspiration this last year in my life. She's humbled me, she's become a close friend and ultimately like family. We've had a few disagreements and differences, but I couldn't have asked for a better friend, poet, and sister to enter this new journey in our lives with."

A few people awed as Karmi placed her hand over her heart and Devin hugged her waist.

"Don't make me cry," Karmi said. "You know it's not something I like to do."

"Well, good thing I have great news."

"Spit it out already!" Amber, who had snuck in while Donnica and Jeremiah were talking, yelled.

Everyone laughed and cosigned.

"Well, not only is Karmi getting married, but later on this

year she'll be an auntie!"

Karmi's face brightened. "You're pregnant? Oh my gosh, I can't wait! I hope it's a girl!" Karmi said, hugging Donnica. She laughed while Devin congratulated Jeremiah. "This is the best news ever," Karmi said but quickly glanced at Devin. "Second best."

"Congratulations!" Langston said, walking over to them. He playfully pushed Karmi's shoulder before leaning over to hug Donnica. "Watch this one; she tries to steal my kid all the time."

They all laughed before standing back to take in the moment.

Donnica was floored by the internal change being with these people had caused. It was the most humbling experience in the world to go from being a bestselling author to blacklisted for a bad attitude and hot temper. She used to pride herself on being so skilled with words, but she knew certain life experiences were so wonderful and divine that she couldn't find words to describe them.

She could try all she wanted to go back into her past and into the internal novels she had written on her future, but she couldn't fathom feeling this good at this very moment.

Her life had unfolded and written itself in faith without her help. That was something she was sure she didn't want to change.

When others accept your story for what it's truly worth, it can make you feel better about your own level of confidence. No matter how much we say we don't care what others think or their opinion of us, acceptance calls to the need to belong somewhere. In the hierarchy of needs, realize that there is nothing wrong with wanting to be loved, just as long as you desire to be loved in the right way.

SNEAK PEEK:
When All Else Fails

Ava's nose flared as she ran through the opening of the kitchen and tackled Bri to the ground. Bri yelled before turning on her back and trying to move Ava off of her. Ava grunted as she slipped her arms under Bri's back and tried to flip her over. Bri shuffled to plant her feet on the ground before pushing forward, knocking Ava on her back onto the gray and black peppered carpet. The action caused the twins to slide up against the cherry wood coffee table, inching it out of its place. Ava smirked, wrapped one of her legs around Bri's waist and used her lower body strength to roll them over. Bri huffed as Ava sat on top of her stomach.

"Ugh get off of me, you whale!" Bri yelled. Ava smiled down at her older sister by mere minutes and wiggled, causing more pain to her. "It was just cereal!"

"No, it was my cereal," Ava said, sticking her tongue out. She smiled as Bri struggled to get under her weight. Over the last two years, Ava had gained a few pounds up on Bri so she knew she'd have a hard time getting out of the position Ava had her in.

"Still acting like kids," Rico said, walking into the living room. He pushed his arms under Ava's, wrapping them around her chest and pulling her off of Bri. Instead of helping his youngest daughter to her feet, Rico unlaced his fingers and Ava fell with a soft thud on her bottom. She scooted next to Bri on the floor and they both laughed.

Rico shook his head as he walked past his daughters and

out of the room.

"I'll buy you some more," Bri said, turning on her belly, pushing her body up on her knees and standing up. Ava shook her head. She could remember when they'd fight about the names Bri called her, how she'd conformed to the ways of the rest of her friends and labeled Ava a whore. They'd fight about how embarrassed Bri was to be Ava's twin, how embarrassed she was of Kita.

Now they fought over cereal.

It was amazing, how different things could be just two years later. If the past events of Ava's life hadn't been so devastatingly relevant to the choices in her present life, they would not seem real. Ava and Bri would be twenty- two soon. High school seemed like a lifetime away, but looking at the relationship she had with her twin now, Ava wasn't mad about it.

The fact that she didn't see Bri much because of her school schedule made Ava always pick on her when she did see her.

"Gelly is the one who's going to be mad at you." "She could never be mad at Ti-Ti B!"

As if hearing her mother and aunt discuss her, three- year-old Angel came toddling through the living room with a dark pink feather duster glued to her hand. Ava watched attentively as her daughter sauntered over to the television stand and proceeded to swipe the duster across the bottom of it.

Bri walked towards the stairs as her cell phone rang while Ava sat up on her elbows and watched Angel.

Her face was less chubby than it had been during her first year of consuming Ava's life. Her eyes still sparkled in dark wonder and her sandy brown curls were beginning to somehow straighten themselves out. Ava loved the dimples that seemed to pop out of nowhere on her child, a trait she would have to attribute to the other half of Angel.

"Gelly, what you doing boo?" Ava asked after a few minutes. When Angel didn't answer, Ava rolled her eyes. "Angel D!"

"What mommy?"

"You heard me, I told you about ignoring mommy."

Angel huffed before giving her mom a sympathetic eye and throwing her hands down. Ava shook her head again. Angel was so much like Ava it was scary.

"Cleanin'."

"You cleaned enough," Ava said, stretching her arms out. Angel dropped the feather duster and walked over to her mom. She stopped at her feet and crawled on her legs to get up to her lap. Ava wrapped her up in her arms and kissed her forehead. Angel was tall for a three-year-old and Ava was almost looking up at her as she sat on her lap. She tried to smooth down the ponytail she'd just done the night before. Ava always joked that she would have hair like Romero's family.

"Go get your shoes and we can go," Ava said, patting Angel on her bottom. Ava's cell phone rang.

Sliding it out of her pocket, she sighed when she saw Dre's name pop up.

"Yo."

"Wow, you actually answered your phone," Dre said.

"I'm sorry, I've been busy," Ava said, pushing herself off the floor.

"I'm doing you a favor yo, I didn't ask you for this opportunity you asked me," Dre said. Ava rolled her eyes at the repetitive threat he gave her.

"I know so who needs a hook?"

"It's a whole song this time, Ava. I need you in tomorrow to go over the idea of it." Ava swallowed the small lump in her throat that formed after 'whole song' left Dre's lips. "Ava, you're still there?"

"I'll be there," she said, before hanging up. Ava sighed before getting Angel and heading out the door to her car.

It had been two years since she stopped singing again but she still wanted to be apart to it. She asked Dre to connect her to some up and coming singers who needed lyrics. The problem was that it didn't pay much at the moment so Ava had to get another job. Between that and taking care of her family, she had missed a lot of the appointments Dre was setting up for her.

It was usually just a chorus or bridge but now Dre wanted her to write full songs. She wondered if she was ready for it, but tomorrow was tomorrow and she didn't have time to think about it.

As Ava turned corners, she looked around in awe. At this point in her life she wasn't sure why she was still in Hamilton, Tennessee and how it could seem so different to her now. A few years before, when she was still in high school, didn't seem like much. Now they had transformed everything around her. She was twenty-one now, things had definitely changed since high school.

Ava smiled as she pulled into her usual parking space next to Sunny's truck. Glancing into the back seat, she saw that Angel was sleeping and smiled harder. Today was Sunny's only day off this week and whenever they came over, he usual spent most of his time playing with Angel.

Ava loved Angel's relationship with Sunny but it would be nice to have a few hours of alone time with him while Angel napped.

Sunny answered the door running his hand down his head, over his low cut fade and his eyes low.

"Get her please," Ava said, trying to shift Angel's weight.

Sunny grunted a little before taking Angel and putting her in his bed. He soon joined Ava on the couch, falling on top of her as she laughed. She knew his job was taking a toll on him. His arms were more defined and the small gut he had was just about gone. His caramel skin had darkened from being out in the sun on different construction sites but Ava fell in love with him all over again after he cut his braids off.

She ran her hand down his fade before he tipped his chin to kiss her lips. Sunny mumbled the words to a song about not knowing her name but loving how good she looked in heels. Ava giggled as she shifted around to get comfortable under his weight.

"I don't even have on heels."

"Don't even matter, baby," Sunny said, pecking her neck. Ava smiled before she closed her eyes. "You always go to sleep on me. I just woke up, I'm not tired anymore."

"Yes you are," Ava said with a sly grin. "Just close your eyes and think about it." She held in a laugh once she heard Sunny suck his teeth.

He was always her center, even before he knew it.

Sunny was cool when Ava was anxious, he was collected when she panicked and level headed when she was going crazy. Sunny was all those things when Ava was all the opposites. The one time she had to be strong for him had connected them for life. Ava never wanted to fall out of love with him.

His breathing evened and Ava smirked as her own slowed down just before she fell asleep.

"It just doesn't feel right today," Ava mumbled, pulling the large headphones off of her ear, allowing her dark curls to fall and frame her face. She tilted her head to the left and the right, waiting on stop type of relief. Her eyes focused outside

of the booth to see one of them glaring at her, one was giving her a disappointed head shake while the other was busy ignoring her.

"What's wrong?"

"Does it sound right?" she asked.

"It sounds a little off. Let's run through it again."

Ava nodded, swallowing a little saliva as her stomach twisted in knots. Quickly exhaling through her nose, she pulled the headphones back over her curls and stepped closer to the suspended microphone.

The walls of the recording booth didn't seem this close to her before. The dark grey padding seemed to be darker and the light was dim. Ava pulled at the neck of her shirt and cleared her throat.

She closed her eyes and tried to sing but none of the notes came out right. She wanted to push through it and get it over with but the track soon stopped, leaving her in silence.

"You're right, it doesn't sound right."

"You sound weird today. I know what you need."

Ava opened her eyes and panicked from not being able to move. She bucked her knees and tried to push what was holding her down. Sunny, jarred from his sleep, jumped up from the couch and looked down at her. Ava sat up crying, looking around and blinking.

"Baby, look at me. You are in my apartment. You were having a nightmare again. You aren't there anymore. I'm here and Angel is in my bed sleeping," Sunny said, grabbing Ava's shoulders to try and calm her down.

"Angel's in your bed sleeping," she repeated as he nodded. Suddenly feeling a need to confirm his assurance, Ava got up from the couch and jogged into Sunny's bedroom. Her heart calmed as she saw Angel curled around one of the pillows. Ava wiped her face with the back of her hands before crawling into the bed and snuggling next to Angel.

Sunny came in minutes later and sighed at the sight of his woman and his little lady. He shook his head before he wiped his face with his hands. Ava had already fallen back to sleep, hugging Angel tightly. He slid in his bed behind her and wrapped his right arm around her waist, protectively.

www.ingramcontent.com/pod-product-compliance
Lightning Source LLC
Chambersburg PA
CBHW071006280626
47160CB00015B/1413